Where had Arthur gone? Maybe if he heard Latin, he'd show himself . . . maybe.

"*Intellectus merces est fidei*," Malcolm called out, hoping he said it correctly. "Understanding is the reward of faith."

Stone grated against stone behind Malcolm. He spun around. The large flat top of the altar moved slightly to the side. Then, with a jerk, it moved further. Arthur kept a watchful eye on Malcolm as he squeezed out of the large coffinlike box and got to his feet.

Arthur slowly reached back into the altar and, in a flash, had his sword out of its sheath and pointed under Malcolm's chin.

"*Veni vedi vici!*"

The unexpected sound of a girl's voice came from a doorway. Arthur turned to see who spoke, just as Jeff and Elizabeth came into the ruins.

"Run, Uncle Malcolm!" Jeff whispered loudly. . . .

Stranger in the Mist

Paul McCusker

LION
PUBLISHING

Lion Publishing
A Division of Cook Communications
4050 Lee Vance View
Colorado Springs, CO 80918, USA

STRANGER IN THE MIST
© 1996 by Paul McCusker

First edition 1996

Cover design by Bill Paetzold
Cover illustration by Matthew Archambault

ISBN 0-7459-3312-1

Printed and bound in the United States of America
00 99 98 97 96   5 4 3 2 1

**Published in association with the literary agency of Alive Communications,
Inc., 1465 Kelly Johnson Blvd., Suite 320, Colorado Springs, CO 80920**

Library of Congress Cataloging-in-Publication Data

McCusker, Paul
        Stranger in the Mist / by Paul McCusker.
                p.   cm. — (Time twists)
        Summary: When King Arthur turns up in America in the mid-1990s,
        fifteen-year-old Elizabeth, Jeff, and Uncle Malcolm decide that they
        must return him to England.
                ISBN (invalid) 0-7459-3312-1
                1. Arthur, King—Juvenile fiction. [1. Arthur, King—Fiction.
        2. Knights and knighthood—Fiction. 3. Time travel—Fiction.
        4. Christian life—Fiction.] I. Title. II. Series: McCusker,
        Paul, 1958- Time twists.
        PZ7.M47841635Su   1996
        [Fic]—dc20   96-17154
                                                          CIP
                                                          AC

With deepest appreciation to the many authors who helped fill in the pieces with their works: Geoffrey Ashe, Henry Gilbert (King Arthur's Knights), Sidney Lanier (The Boy's King Arthur), Ronan Coghlan (The Encyclopedia of Arthurian Legends), and Kenneth McLeish (Myths and Folk Stories of Britain and Ireland). I'm also grateful to the staff members of the British Embassy in Washington, D.C. and the British Consulate in Denver, Philip Glassborow, Ruth and Gareth Mayers, and, mostly, my wife Elizabeth, who shared the joy of that first image of King Arthur being knocked off of a horse on the motorway.

"Quid est ergo tempus? si nemo ex me quaerat, scio; si quaerenti explicare velim, nescio." ("What, then, is time? If no one asks me, I know; if I want to explain it to someone who does ask me, I do not know.")

St. Augustine

A tall, gray old man stepped to the pinnacle of Glastonbury Tor, an unusual conelike hill on which stood a tower named for a saint. In the wet English twilight, the wind whipped the old man's long gray hair and beard and his ragged brown monk's robe like a flag in a gale. The dark clouds above moved and gathered as if they thought him a curiosity worth investigating. Chalice Hill and Wearyall Hill waited in attendance nearby, their shoulders hunched like two old porters. The battered abbey beyond Chalice Hill listened in silence, unable to see from its skewered position.

The old man, a soloist before a strange orchestra, cast a sad eye to the green quilt littered with small houses and shops. They were an indifferent audience.

The old man prayed silently for a moment, then pulled an old curved horn from under his habit. He placed it to his lips and blew once, then twice, then a third time. The three muted blasts were caught by the wind and carried away.

The overture was finished, the program was just beginning.

"Look at that," Ben Hearn said to his wife, Kathryn. "It's crazy, I tell you. Crazy."

They were in Ben's pickup truck rattling toward Fawlt Line High School to help chaperon the sophomore class end-of-the-year dance. Mr. and Mrs. Hearn weren't keen on dances themselves, but their daughter Chelsea would be there for her first real dance in a formal dress and flowers and carefully permed hair.

"Kathryn, are you listening to me?"

"What's crazy, Ben?" Kathryn suddenly asked, peering through the unusual fog.

"Didn't you see the sign for Malcolm Dubbs's village?"

Kathryn hadn't. But they were on one of the roads bordering the vast Dubbs estate, and she knew what sign her husband was talking about. It was the one that announced the construction of Malcolm Dubbs's Historical Village.

"I don't know what the town council was thinking when they agreed to it," Ben said. Malcolm was the most wealthy citizen of their little town of Fawlt Line. In fact, his family had been there for close to two centuries. Malcolm, a history buff, had designated a large portion of his property for the village.

Kathryn squinted at the fog ahead. "Don't you think you should slow down? It's getting thicker."

The truck engine whined as Ben heeded his wife. "You know what he's doing with the village, right? He's shipping in *buildings*. Brick by brick and stone by stone from all over the world. Have you ever heard of such a thing? A museum with a few trinkets and artifacts I could understand, but buildings?"

Kathryn smiled. "Malcolm always was obsessed with history. I remember when we were in school together—"

Ben wasn't listening. "Do you know what they've been working on for the past few weeks? Some kind of a ruin from England. A monastery or castle or cathedral, I don't know for sure."

"From England?" Kathryn asked, instantly lost in the romance of the idea. Then she grinned. "Did he have this fog shipped in too?"

Ben grunted, "I just don't understand Malcolm's fascination with something that's ruined. What's the point?"

Kathryn was about to answer—and would have—if a man on horseback hadn't suddenly appeared on the road in front of them. The fog cleared just in time for Ben to see him, mutter an oath as he hit the brakes, and jerk the steering wheel to the right. The horse reared wildly, and the rider flew backward to the ground. Kathryn cried out as the truck skidded into a ditch on the side of the road and came to a gravel-spraying stop. Ben and Kathryn looked at each other shakily.

"You all right?" Ben asked.

Kathryn nodded.

"Of all the stupid things to do—" Ben growled and angrily pushed his door open. The angle of the truck threatened to spring it back on him. He pushed harder and held it in place as he crawled out. "Stay here," he said before the door slammed shut again.

Kathryn reached over and turned on the emergency flashers.

The on-and-off yellow light barely penetrated the fog that swirled around Ben's feet. He made his way cautiously down the road. "Fool," Ben muttered to himself, then called out. "Hello? Are you all right?"

The fog parted as if to show Ben the man lying on the side of the road.

"Oh no," Ben said, rushing forward. He crouched down next to the figure, which seemed to be wrapped in a dark blanket. He was perfectly still. Even in the darkness, Ben could tell he was a bear of a man. His face was hidden in the fog and shadows.

"Hey," Ben said, hoping the man would stir. Ben looked him over for any sign of blood. Nothing was obvious around his head. But what could he expect to see in the darkness? "Kathryn!" he shouted back toward the car. "Bring me the flashlight from the glove compartment!"

He peered closely at the shadowed form of the man as he heard Kathryn open her door. *What's the guy doing in a blanket? Why's he riding a horse so late in the evening? Why would anyone dash across a road thick with fog?* The crunch of his wife's shoes on the gravel came closer. The shaft of light from the flashlight bounced around eerily in the ever moving fog.

Kathryn joined him and beamed the light at the stranger. He had long dark salt-and-pepper hair, beard, and mustache and a rugged, outdoorsy kind of face. Anywhere from forty to sixty years old, Ben figured. He wore a peaceful expression. He could've been sleeping.

"He's not dead, is he?" Kathryn asked, reacting in her own way to the peculiar serenity on the man's face.

"I don't think so." Ben reached down, separating the blanket to check the man's vital signs. The feel of the cloth told him it wasn't a blanket at all. As he pushed the fabric aside, he realized that it was a cape made of a thick coarse material, clasped at the neck by a dragon brooch. "What in the world—?"

Kathryn gasped.

They expected to see a shirt or a sweater or a coat of some sort. Instead the man wore a long vest with the symbol of a dragon stitched on the front, a gold belt, brown leggings, and soft leather footwear that looked more like slippers than shoes. The whole outfit reminded Ben of a costume in a Robin Hood movie. At the stranger's side was a sword in a sheath.

"Is it Halloween?" Kathryn asked.

Ben shook his head. "I think I'd better get the truck out of that ditch so you can go for help."

At the high school, the dance was just getting under way. The Starliners, a band from nearby Hancock, warmed up for their first number as the sound engineer tried to get the volume just right. The speakers screamed feedback at the impatient sophomores.

Jeff Dubbs, dressed in a tux and looking all the more uncomfortable for it, stepped into the converted gymnasium and stopped for a look around. Streamers and balloons blew gently in the rafters above. A banner wishing the returning class a good summer rustled over the scoreboard.

A couple dozen kids mingled in the middle of the dance floor and along the walls. Jeff tugged at his collar and wished he were somewhere else. Anywhere else.

Elizabeth Forde, his longtime-friend-turned-girlfriend, slipped her hand into the crook of his arm. "Tell me you like it. We were here all afternoon getting the room decorated."

"It's nice," Jeff said. *You're nicer,* he thought as he looked Elizabeth over for the umpteenth time. She was wearing a stunning pink gown with lots of lacy things around the neck and sleeves. The white corsage he had bought for her was pinned to the strap. She looked out over the gathering students, and he took in her profile: the delicate nose, large brown eyes, full lips, all framed by long brown hair that she'd taken extra care with that evening. He had to admit it, she was beautiful.

She glanced over and caught him looking at her. He blushed.

"What's wrong?" she asked self-consciously.

A loud crash behind them saved Jeff from answering. Elizabeth's father, Alan Forde, an eccentric man at the best of times, had dropped a tray of paper cups filled with drinks. Elizabeth's mother rolled her eyes. "I told you to be careful."

"Too many cups to one side," he answered quickly as he knelt to clean up the mess. "I misjudged the balance."

"Oh, Daddy," said Elizabeth, bemused, and went to help.

Jeff smiled. There was a time when Elizabeth would have raced from the room in embarrassment over her father. Not now. Not since she'd had an adventure that made her realize, among other things, how much she loved her parents, quirks and all.

"Hello, Jeff," Malcolm Dubbs said, just arriving through the main doors. Malcolm was Jeff's uncle and had been his guardian since his parents were killed a couple of years before.

"Hi, Uncle Malcolm," Jeff said. "Nice suit. Haven't seen that one before."

Malcolm tugged at the bottom of his jacket. "It doesn't smell like mothballs, does it?"

Jeff sniffed the air. "Nope."

"Good."

The lead singer for the band stepped up to the microphone. "Hello, everybody. How're you doing? We're the Starliners, and we hope you're ready to dance!" The three-piece brass section started an up-tempo song with the rest of the band joining in a few bars later. A handful of dancers wiggled their way onto the floor. Again, Jeff wished he were somewhere else.

Elizabeth left her father and mother to finish cleaning up the spilled drinks and rejoined Jeff.

"You look exquisite, Elizabeth," Malcolm said.

"Thank you, Uncle Malcolm." Elizabeth curtsied. "You look pretty nice yourself."

He smiled at her, then at Jeff. "Why don't you two dance?"

"Uncle Malcolm," Jeff said through clenched teeth. Malcolm knew how Jeff felt about dancing.

Elizabeth feigned a melodramatic tone. "I've resigned myself to an evening as a wallflower. My escort doesn't dance."

"Aw, we can't let a little thing like that get in the way," Malcolm said. "Will you dance with me?"

"I'd love to," she said and offered him her hand.

He took it and winked at Jeff as he led her onto the dance floor. Jeff leaned against the door post, his arms folded. Upstaged by his uncle once again. But he didn't really mind.

A tap on the shoulder took his gaze from the dance floor into the round boyish face of Sheriff Richard Hounslow. The sheriff's shirt was unbuttoned at the collar, and his only equipment was his badge and a walkie-talkie strapped to his belt. Sheriff Hounslow didn't wear a gun unless he had to. "Is your uncle here?" he asked.

Jeff tipped his head toward the dance floor. "Out there with Elizabeth. Is something wrong?"

"Kinda."

"You want me to get him?"

Hounslow shook his head. "Wait until the song's over."

They stood silently and watched Malcolm and Elizabeth play Fred Astaire and Ginger Rogers amidst the wild gyrations of the dancers around them.

"He's not bad," Hounslow said.

The song ended, and Uncle Malcolm and Elizabeth, pleasantly breathless, returned to Jeff.

"Uh-oh," Malcolm said when he saw Hounslow. "What's wrong?"

Hounslow straightened up. "I need you to come to the hospital. Apparently one of the workers from your historical village was knocked down by Ben Hearn's truck." He said the words "historical village" with a solid note of sarcasm.

"One of my workers?" Malcolm said, surprised. "But they're off for the weekend. Are you sure he's from my village?"

Hounslow shrugged. "He came racing off your property on a horse and ran right in front of Ben. Worse, he doesn't speak a word of English, just some gibberish. That's why I need you to come."

"Is he seriously hurt?"

"No, but Doc McConnell wants to keep him overnight for observation." Hounslow gestured to the dance. "Sorry to take you away from the fun."

"Hmm." Malcolm tugged his ear thoughtfully, then turned to Jeff. "I leave Elizabeth in your capable hands. Dance with her."

Jeff hung his head.

"You heard your uncle," Elizabeth said and dragged Jeff onto the dance floor.

The stranger had caused such a ruckus at the hospital—shouting, trying to get away—that the doctor had had to sedate him and put him in a private room. He lay sleeping as Malcolm, Sheriff Hounslow, and Dr. McConnell approached the bed.

"We had to give him three times the normal dose because of his size," Dr. McConnell said.

Malcolm looked closely at the unconscious figure. He was big, all right, stretching the length of the bed. "I'd certainly remember this man if he worked on my village," Malcolm said. "I've never seen him before."

"He was riding one of your horses," Hounslow stated.

Malcolm cocked an eyebrow. "I'll have to talk to Mr. Farrar, my groundskeeper. He lives in the cottage next to the stables."

"Already done," Hounslow said. "He was watching television. Didn't hear a thing. So, if nothing else, you could press charges against the man for horse thievery."

Malcolm shook his head. "I'd like to find out more about him first."

"Good luck. We couldn't get anything out of him. He kept yakking away in some gibberish. Pounded his chest and called himself 'Rex' or 'Regis' or something like that."

Dr. McConnell interjected, "I had time to think about it after we got him sedated. He spoke words and phrases that reminded me of the Latin I picked up in medical school."

"Latin?"

"*Old* Latin, I think," Dr. McConnell said. "But I'm no expert."

Hounslow pulled at his belt. "I called the mental hospital in Grantsville to see if they've had any escapes. Nothing."

"Just because he speaks Latin doesn't mean he's mentally disturbed," Malcolm said.

"Granted," Hounslow answered. "But how about that?" He pointed to the stranger's clothes, now draped across a chair.

Malcolm couldn't mask his surprise. "This is what he was wearing?"

Hounslow nodded. "That's another reason we figured he was from your village."

"The construction workers are still building," Malcolm said. "I haven't hired any staff yet." He fingered the fabric of the robe and tunic, making a mental note of the dragon insignias. He picked up the soft leather shoes and looked them over. "Amazing. The outfit looks so authentic. And I don't mean authentic like a well-done replica. These things look *worn*, like real clothes."

"What do you mean?" Dr. McConnell asked.

"I mean, they're worn out in the same way that clothes we wear regularly would look worn. Not like a costume that someone might put on once or twice a year."

"Maybe he's one of those homeless fruitcakes who just happened to wander into town," Hounslow offered.

Dr. McConnell folded his arms. "Though it's hard to imagine this guy being homeless and just wandering about with that sword."

"Sword?"

"I forgot to mention it," Hounslow said and opened the door of the large wooden wardrobe in the corner. With both hands he pulled out a long sword encased in an ornate golden scabbard. He cradled it in his arms for Malcolm to inspect.

"Good grief," Malcolm gasped, running his hand along the golden scabbard. "Is that real gold?"

"Looks like it," Hounslow said.

Malcolm examined the handle of the sword, also golden with a row of unfamiliar jewels imbedded along the length of the stem. Even in the washed-out fluorescent light of the room, they sparkled as if they reflected the sun. "Can I take it out?"

"Yeah," Hounslow said, "but be careful. It's heavy and *sharp*."

Malcolm grabbed the handle with both hands and withdrew the sword from the scabbard. It was heavy, as the sheriff had said, and Malcolm imagined it would take a man the size of the stranger to wield it with any effect. It was a strain just to hold it up. The blade was made of thick, shiny steel with an elaborate engraving of what looked like thin vines and blossoms along the edges. "It must be worth a fortune," Malcolm said as he slid the sword back into the sheath.

Dr. McConnell agreed. "So what's a derelict doing with a Latin vocabulary and a sword of that value?"

"That's what I'd like to find out when he wakes up," Malcolm answered.

CHAPTER 2

Within two hours the stranger was awake and pulling at the restraining straps on the bed. He shouted at the nurse, Dr. McConnell, Sheriff Hounslow, and Malcolm in a tone that was unmistakably belligerent. He alternately yanked at the straps, yelled at everyone present, or resigned himself to watching the flashing lights and electronic graphs on the medical equipment around him.

After hearing a few of the phrases he yelled—like *rex, regis, libertas, stultus*—Malcolm was certain about the Latin and phoned a friend of his from the university at Frostburg.

Dr. Camilla Ashe was so intrigued by Malcolm's description that she decided not to wait until morning, and drove the forty-five minutes to Fawlt Line that night. She arrived a little after nine. By that time the group in the room included Jerry Anderson, editor of Fawlt Line's *Daily Gazette*. He had heard the news about the mystery man on his police scanner.

Dr. Ashe, a prim, scholarly woman dressed in tweeds, approached the side of the bed warily. The stranger, transfixed by the lights on the equipment, only realized she was there when she cleared her throat. He looked at her with an expression of impatience—until she spoke to him in Latin. His mouth fell open with surprise. Then, realizing he finally had someone to communicate with, he bombarded her with words. His voice rose to a shout, and she responded in kind. It looked and sounded like a full-blown argument.

Malcolm watched them, wishing he had taken the time to study Latin in college. Maybe he would make that his summer project.

While the exchange between Dr. Ashe and the stranger was going on, Jeff and Elizabeth quietly slipped into the room, still dressed for the dance. They leaned against the far wall, out of the way.

16

The stranger continued his assault with words. Finally, Dr. Ashe put her hands on her hips and spoke in a tone that was withering in any language. The stranger turned his head away from her as if to say that the conversation was over. He didn't look at her again. She spun around to the expectant group, growled loudly, and stormed out of the room.

"What was that all about?" Malcolm asked, catching up with her in the hall.

Her hands trembled as she unwrapped a piece of gum and tossed it into her mouth. "I gave up smoking," she said as if Malcolm had asked her about the gum. "I'd love a cigarette now."

"Sorry," Malcolm said, and waited politely for her to compose herself.

"He said he didn't want to talk to a woman," she said. "He resented a woman being sent to him by his captors."

"Captors!"

Dr. Ashe chewed her gum forcefully. "I don't mind saying that that man should be certified. He's not sane."

"Why? What did he say?"

"He said that as a king, he should be treated with more respect. He wants to speak with whichever baron or duke is holding him captive. He wants to know where he's being held and if there's a ransom. He demands to be told how he got here and where his knights are. And, finally, he wants someone to tell him about the magic boxes with the flashing lights."

"I told you he's a fruitcake," Sheriff Hounslow said from behind Malcolm.

"Or this is a very tiresome joke," Dr. Ashe replied and wagged a finger at Malcolm. "You wouldn't be pulling a prank on me, would you?"

"No," Malcolm said simply.

"Then you should get him some psychiatric help," she said.

"I still don't understand," Malcolm said. "He says he's a king. King Who?—and of what?"

Dr. Ashe grinned irritably. "He says he's King Arthur."

CHAPTER 3

Dr. Ashe left. She wanted nothing more to do with a Latin-speaking lunatic who thought he was King Arthur.

"What are you going to do now?" Jerry Anderson asked Malcolm.

Before Malcolm could answer, Hounslow jumped in. "Let's get something straight. Doc McConnell and I are making the decisions here. Not Malcolm."

"Sorry," Jerry said. "What are you going to do now, Sheriff Hounslow?"

Hounslow shrugged. "I don't know yet."

Malcolm politely smiled. "In my humble opinion, we should find someone else who knows enough Latin to communicate with him. But who?"

Elizabeth spoke from her corner. "I know someone."

All eyes turned to her, and she swallowed self-consciously. "My dad. He studied Latin in college and sometimes uses it for his research." Elizabeth's father was a teacher at the middle school, though some said he should have been teaching at a university.

"I should have thought of it first," Malcolm said and went to the phone.

Alan Forde arrived quickly. He was quite tall himself, and the combination of his size and his knowledge of Latin seemed to impress the stranger, who grew more patient and willing to talk. Alan pulled up a chair next to the bed. After a brief conversation, he turned to Dr. McConnell. "May we free his hands, please?"

Dr. McConnell looked skeptically at Alan and the stranger. "You're kidding."

"He promises not to resort to physical violence or even to attempt an escape. But it's offensive to his honor to be tied up."

"Well . . ." Dr. McConnell began, then looked to Sheriff Hounslow and Malcolm for help.

"I think you should do it," Malcolm suggested.

Sheriff Hounslow unclipped the walkie-talkie from his belt and called to one of his officers on the other end. "Bring me my gun," he ordered, and the officer did.

"Okay," Dr. McConnell said. He undid the restraining straps. The stranger rubbed his wrists, sat up, and spoke to Alan.

"Thank you," Alan translated. The interview began.

"Does he really think he's King Arthur?" Hounslow asked.

"Yes."

"Then what's he doing here? What was he doing on my property? Why did he take my horse?" Malcolm asked.

Alan held up his hand. "Please, Malcolm. A little at a time." He then posed the questions to the stranger.

Through Alan, the stranger explained, "My nephew Sir Mordred, that traitorous and wicked knight, attempted to usurp my throne while I was pursuing Sir Lancelot north to his castle. I loved Lancelot as my own, even while he coveted my queen and betrayed me. While I was gone, Mordred enticed many weak-willed nobles to join him. My army met and routed his forces on Barham Down, but he fled to other parts. We made chase but did not battle them again, choosing instead to negotiate a peace. I did not desire the terrible bloodshed that would ensue if we were to fight. And so we came to the plain to meet and discuss terms."

"What's this got to do with anything?" Hounslow growled.

Malcolm waved him off. "So tonight is the eve of your meeting with Mordred to make a truce," he said to Alan while looking at the stranger. "What happened?"

Again Alan interpreted the stranger's reply: "As I lay upon my bed in my pavilion, I dreamed an incredible dream. I sat upon a chair that was fastened to a wheel in the sky. I was adorned in a garment of finest woven gold. Far below me I saw deep black water containing serpents and worms and the most foul and horrible wild beasts. All of a sudden, the wheel turned upside down. I fell among the serpents and wild beasts, and they pounced on me. I cried out and awoke upon a cold slab of stone in the middle of a vast field. Troubled by this vision, I rose determined to find my knights. I saw glowing torches in the distance and approached them. I found there not my army, but a stable of horses. I mounted one and, following the stars, made haste in the direction of my knights. I spurred the horse ever faster until I was attacked by an armored cart drawn by neither man nor beast. Frightened, my horse reared upon its hind legs, and I fell to the ground. Now tell me, knave," he concluded, directing the question to Malcolm, "am I a prisoner or is this still a dream?"

Malcolm tugged at his ear. "He woke up on one of the stone slabs in my historical village. Probably in the church ruins I bought from England. Very interesting."

"You don't believe any of this nonsense, do you?" Hounslow asked.

Malcolm answered in a guarded tone. "For the moment I believe that he's confused and found himself on my property."

The stranger folded his arms and muttered the same phrase over and over.

"He says Merlin is responsible," Alan said. "He doesn't know how, but he's sure it is some trickery of Merlin's."

"That's it," Hounslow said. "Everybody out. It's nearly eleven, and I've had enough of this nonsense. We're going to transfer this nut case to the psych ward at Hancock. Let them decide what to do with him!" He marched out of the room.

Dr. McConnell looked at Malcolm apologetically and shrugged. "What else can I do?"

Malcolm didn't know. "I wish I could take him back to my cottage."

The stranger spoke again, and Alan translated, "Answer me! Am I to be ransomed or is this a dream?"

Malcolm spoke as soothingly as he could. "Tell him that we are not his captors and, if it'll help, to consider this a bizarre dream." As an afterthought, he added, "Also ask him if he'll give us his word as king not to try to escape tonight. Otherwise, the doctor will have to strap his arms again."

Arthur gave his word.

CHAPTER 4

The next morning Malcolm sat at the breakfast table deeply immersed in the legend of King Arthur. Jeff dropped the *Daily Gazette* in front of him. IS HE OR ISN'T HE? MAN CLAIMS TO BE KING ARTHUR the headline shouted in large type. Malcolm glanced at it, then returned to his book. "Front page, huh? I guess Jerry figured it was more exciting than the proposed resurfacing of Union Street."

"Uncle Malcolm?" Jeff sat down on the chair next to him. "Do you really think this guy is King Arthur? I mean, I know better than anyone that weird things happen around here. But King Arthur—in Fawlt Line? Why?"

Malcolm gazed at his young nephew. "Beats me. That's why I'm refreshing myself on Arthurian legends. Maybe there's a clue in here somewhere."

Jeff sighed. "Unless the guy really is out of his mind."

"Of course," Malcolm said without conviction. "But if he's crazy, he knows his Arthur. Everything he described is in these books."

"Like what?"

"All of it. Mordred, who really was a slime-bucket, tried to take over the kingdom while Arthur was out of the country chasing Lancelot. Arthur came back to fight him, and they met on Salisbury Plain for a final battle." Malcolm turned the book on the table so Jeff could see it. He pointed to the facing page. "This is interesting. Some of the legends include the dream he told us about. Apparently it was so horrific he cried out, and his knights came rushing in. He told them what he had seen, and his advisors said it was symbolic. Mordred would kill him in battle. They advised him to negotiate an agreement rather than fight. Arthur reluctantly agreed."

"Then what?"

"They met on the field to talk terms," Malcolm continued, "but the understanding was if any of the attending soldiers pulled out a weapon for any reason, then they'd battle. Legend has it that just as Arthur and Mordred came to an agreement about peace, a snake slithered over the foot of one of the knights. He instinctively pulled out his sword to kill it. At the sight of the sword, Mordred cried out that it was a trick and called his men to attack. A slaughter followed."

"Who won?"

"Nobody."

Jeff frowned. "Nobody?"

"Mordred fatally wounded Arthur, and Arthur killed Mordred. And that's where the legends split off into two different endings. One legend has Arthur dying and being buried somewhere, although no one can agree where. Most say it was in a town called Glastonbury. Supposedly King Henry II found his body there during his reign."

"What's the other legend say?"

"That his body was taken away in a magical boat by the Lady of the Lake and her attendants."

Jeff smiled. "The Lady of the Lake?"

Malcolm looked at his nephew impatiently. "The lady who gave him the sword Excalibur. Don't you even know the basics of the story?"

"Nope. I thought Excalibur was the sword he pulled out of the stone."

"No, the sword in the stone was the one that revealed that Arthur was king. Excalibur was given to him later." Malcolm shoved the books at him. "Your assignment for the day is to get familiar with the legend of Arthur."

"Hey, I'm out of school!" Jeff complained.

"We're never out of school, Jeff," Malcolm replied.

Mrs. Packer, their housekeeper, came into the room to retrieve the dirty breakfast dishes. "I assume that both of you scholars know the rest of the legend," she said as she loaded the tray with plates and cups.

"Please tell me," Malcolm said.

"As you know, I am of English descent," she began. "When I was a child, my grandmother told me stories of Arthur. One thing she said again and again was that Arthur would return one day. The once and future king."

Jeff looked at his uncle. "What?"

"Didn't you know? They said he would return at Britain's greatest time of need." She adjusted the tray on her hand. "I guess they gave up on that notion after Hitler and his bombing blitz on London. That's when Britain needed him the most, I suppose." She spun on her heels and left the room.

Malcolm leaned back in his chair. "You realize, of course, that if he's really Arthur, then we're dealing with a man who has risen from the dead to be here."

"But he's no ghost," Jeff said. "You saw him. He's flesh and blood."

Malcolm nodded. "That's the thing I can't stop thinking about. He's here in the flesh. How is that possible?"

"You think he somehow slipped through time?" Jeff asked.

Malcolm patted Jeff's arm. "You're the one with the time travel experience. Why don't you tell me?"

Before Jeff could answer, the phone rang. He grabbed it. "Hello?" He listened for a minute, mumbled a quick thanks, and hung up. "Uh-oh."

Malcolm looked at him.

"Arthur escaped from the hospital this morning when they were putting him in a van to take him to Hancock. They said he tossed two of the policemen into a dumpster. He got his clothes and sword from the front of the cab, and ran off through the field behind the hospital."

"Anybody hurt?"

"No," Jeff answered. "So much for a king's word."

Malcolm smiled and spoke as if he had known it would happen. "He promised not to try to escape last night. He didn't say anything about this morning."

CHAPTER 5

Sheriff Hounslow didn't like disruptions to his day. Particularly when the disruptions involved racing around the countryside looking for a large lunatic with a king complex and a very long sword.

He grabbed his handset and barked, "Anybody see anything?"

The radio spat static back at him, and then his men reported "negative" from points around town.

"Okay. Keep your eyes peeled. I'm on Rangewood Road on the south side of the Dubbs property heading toward—*Holy Mackerel! There he is!*" Hounslow nearly drove off the road at the sight of Arthur on horseback galloping across Malcolm's land.

"What was that, Sheriff?" someone asked.

"He's on horseback! On Malcolm's property! Surround the place right now!" Hounslow threw the handset down and turned the car onto the first level spot of land he could find. It was enough of a path to get him in the right direction. The car bounced around like a bucking bronco. He fumbled for the switch to turn on the lights and sirens.

Arthur spurred the horse toward the church ruins about two hundred yards ahead. Hounslow did his best to keep up. His car wasn't made for such a rough terrain. He heard his men shouting on the radio but didn't dare take his hands off the wheel to pick up the handset to respond. Suddenly Hounslow's car hopped from the grassy field to a service road that seemed to appear magically in front of him. He laughed confidently to himself as the space between himself and Arthur lessened.

Grabbing the handset he yelled, "He's headed for the church ruins at the center of the village!"

The church ruins were actually four stone walls and a makeshift roof, enclosed by a wooden construction barricade. Even with the barricade, Hounslow thought the ruins looked more like part of a cathedral than a church, since all he knew of churches were the traditional American kind.

Malcolm had purchased the ruin from a financially troubled parish in England—why was beyond Hounslow's imagination. Malcolm was quoted in the *Gazette* as saying that he hoped to restore the church to the way it looked hundreds of years ago.

Hounslow saw Arthur reign in his horse, leap off, and disappear beyond the construction barricades. The sheriff didn't fail to notice the sword swinging at his quarry's side. He brought his car to a skidding stop on the loose gravel, scanned the area, and considered his options. He could wait for the rest of his force or go in on his own. He opted for the latter, checking the bullets in his gun before he got out of the car.

The sun shone brightly. Sweat formed on Hounslow's brow as he approached the ruin. He carefully rounded the corner of the barricade, keeping in mind the length of the sword should the madman decide to swing it at him. Hounslow moved past the entrance to an arched open doorway. The large wooden door leaned against the stone wall, waiting to be fitted. Hounslow gingerly stepped inside. It was cool and smelled of damp moss. Light streamed through the large, unfinished spaces in the ancient roof, but it didn't help Hounslow to see any better. There were enough shadowed nooks and crannies to keep him on edge.

I should have waited for backup, he thought as he looked at the two rows of fat round pillars extending through the church. Arthur could leap out from behind any one of them.

"Okay, pal," Hounslow called out, "just give yourself up, and no one'll get hurt." He didn't know why he spoke at all. It was pointless if this guy really didn't understand English.

Slowly he made his way further into the main sanctuary—the nave, as it was called—and looked around. Stones and workers' debris were scattered everywhere. Hounslow noticed that the church actually had small slots for windows, now boarded up. A large blackbird squawked at him from one of the sills, then flapped noisily until it disappeared through an unfinished part of the south wall.

He looked left and right, his eyes darting quickly to catch any sign of movement in the shadows. His hard heels alternately brushed and clicked against the dirt-covered stone floor. He walked to the far end of the church and stopped in the area where he figured the altar belonged. There in the center sat a large stone block with a slab on top.

He was relieved to hear a car pull up outside, then another. A third soon joined them. Car doors slammed and heavy feet crunched toward him on the gravel.

"Sheriff!"

"Inside!" Hounslow shouted back. "Circle the building, then carefully make your way to the center. And keep your guns handy!"

Within a minute, Hounslow's patrols were coming toward him from four different entrances, guns poised to shoot. They looked at each other and shrugged.

"He has to be around here somewhere," Hounslow said. "Keep looking."

They dispersed as Hounslow checked the perimeter to see if it were possible for Arthur to have raced to any nearby woods. But there were no nearby woods that he could have raced to without being seen. Officer Brendan came out of the shadows of the ruins and flinched at the sunlight.

"Well?" Hounslow asked.

"Nothing, Sheriff," Brendan said. "No sign of him."

Hounslow slapped the stone wall. "He couldn't just disappear."

Malcolm approached in his jeep. He pulled up next to Hounslow and got out. "What's going on, Sheriff?"

"I tracked our mad king to your church here," Hounslow said.

"So where is he?"

Hounslow looked annoyed. "I don't know. He ran inside and vanished."

"Vanished," Malcolm repeated with mock skepticism.

"Don't start with me, Malcolm. I don't want a lecture on your theories about time travel and all that junk." He waved at his officers. "Search the grounds!"

One by one the officers returned to their cars and drove off in separate directions on the network of service roads through Malcolm's village.

"I assume you'll let me know if he shows up," Hounslow said as he got into his car.

"Eventually," Malcolm said with a smile.

Hounslow shook his head. "He's dangerous, Malcolm. He's not another pet project for you to toy with, like some kind of a rat in a cage."

"I don't put things in cages," Malcolm said. "What were you going to do with him?"

Hounslow snorted and drove away.

Malcolm walked to the center of the ruin and looked around. Where had Arthur gone, he wondered. If he were hiding around here somewhere, how could Malcolm draw him out? He remembered a Latin quote from St. Augustine he had learned in college. Maybe if Arthur heard Latin, he'd show himself . . . maybe.

"Intellectus merces est fidei," Malcolm called out, hoping he said it correctly. *Understanding is the reward of faith.* He waited a moment, then said again, *"Intellectus merces est fidei."*

Stone grated against stone behind Malcolm. He spun around. The large flat top of the altar moved slightly to the side. Then, with a jerk, it moved further. Malcolm grinned appreciatively. He grabbed the edge of the top and pushed to help make enough room for Arthur to sit up. Arthur kept a watchful eye on Malcolm as he squeezed out of the large coffinlike box and got to his feet.

"Good for you!" Malcolm exclaimed, glad to see him safe. "Smart thinking!"

Arthur stood on the opposite side of the altar from Malcolm with a stern expression on his face. He said something in Latin.

Malcolm gestured to show that he didn't understand.

Arthur slowly reached back into the altar and, in a flash, had his sword out of its sheath and pointed under Malcolm's chin.

"Veni vedi vici!"

The unexpected sound of a girl's voice came from a doorway. Malcolm looked past Arthur in astonishment. Arthur turned to see who spoke, just as Jeff and Elizabeth came into the ruins.

"Run, Uncle Malcolm!" Jeff whispered loudly in his best effort to sound as if he weren't whispering loudly.

"E pluribus unum!" Elizabeth shouted at Arthur.

Arthur tilted his head like a dog who'd heard a high-pitched whistle. Then he laughed. A chuckle, at first, then a full, boisterous laugh, with his head tipped back. He let the sword drop away. Relieved, Malcolm slumped against the stone altar.

"What in the world was that?" Malcolm asked Elizabeth.

"I thought shouting at him in Latin might give you a chance to run," she explained from a safe distance. "It's all I could think of."

Relaxed now, Arthur sheathed his sword and spoke. They looked at him questioningly. He furrowed his brow as if he realized how futile it was to speak to them. Then he pointed to the door and waved his hands to shoo them away.

"I wonder if we can get him back to the house," Malcolm said. He followed the statement with a variety of gestures designed to persuade Arthur to come with them.

Arthur folded his arms and shook his head in reply. He shooed them away again.

"We can't leave him here," Malcolm said impatiently. *"We can't leave you here!"* he shouted at Arthur, as if increasing his volume would make the man understand.

Arthur pointed at the door.

"What are we going to do?" Jeff asked.

Elizabeth bravely stepped toward Arthur and held out her hand. *"Venite, filia,"* she said.

Arthur's expression softened as he looked at her face, her outstretched hand, then her face again. He smiled and slowly enveloped her hand with his.

With a nervous glance at Jeff and Malcolm, she led him out of the ruins into the golden sunlight.

"What did you say to him?" Jeff asked as he and Malcolm followed them out.

"Something my dad used to say to me," she answered. "Come, child." She frowned. "Well, I think that's what it meant. I may have just called him my daughter."

Outside, the three of them climbed into the jeep. Arthur stopped several feet away from it. They beckoned him in. He shook his head no.

"Oh, brother," Malcolm sighed, as he started the engine.

Arthur circled it several times, jabbing parts of it with his hand, looking under it, cautiously touching the tires and doors, then giving it several pushes that were enough to give the vehicle a good rocking. His face was alive with curiosity.

"Well? Is it safe enough for you?" Malcolm asked.

Arthur ran his hand along the steering wheel. He seemed to enjoy the way the tires moved when he turned it one way and the other. He pushed on the center, and the horn let out a loud blast.

Instantly, Arthur's sword was out, ready to run the beast through.

"No! No!" the three of them yelled.

Arthur put his sword away and walked over to Malcolm's horse, still waiting patiently by the side of the church ruins. He climbed on and waved Malcolm ahead.

"I guess he wants to follow us," Jeff said.

Malcolm put the jeep into gear and away they went.

As they drove, Elizabeth called her father on the cellular phone and asked him to meet them at Malcolm's cottage. "But make sure the police don't follow you," she added before she hung up.

Malcolm nodded his approval. "You're a bright girl."

At Malcolm's cottage, Arthur's inquisitive inspection started all over again. He marveled at the relationship between the switch on the wall and the light on the table. He rifled through Malcolm's books and stared openmouthed at Malcolm's computer.

Jeff turned on the television, and Arthur was nearly apoplectic from the vision and sound. Jeff showed him how the remote control changed the channels. A big mistake. Arthur took it and switched quickly from station to station over and over again.

"A born channel surfer," Jeff said.

Arthur settled on a news program.

"A *boring* channel surfer," Jeff amended.

Arthur watched for a moment, then suddenly jumped up and looked behind the TV. He looked at the front, then the back again.

"What's he doing?" Jeff asked.

Malcolm shrugged. "I couldn't begin to guess."

Alan Forde arrived and, after giving Elizabeth a rough kiss on the cheek, said hello to Arthur in Latin. Arthur seemed to remember Alan and immediately besieged him with questions.

"He wants to know where the rest of the little man is," Alan laughed. "He can see the front of him, but can't figure out why he can't see the back of him."

Arthur grabbed Alan's arm and led him around the room, pointing to various things for him to explain.

While they were preoccupied, Malcolm called for Mrs. Packer.

"Yes, sir?" she asked, but she kept her sights on Arthur.

"I'd like you to—"

"Aren't you going to introduce me?"

Malcolm was taken aback, but signaled Alan to bring Arthur over. "Alan, please introduce Mrs. Packer to his lordship."

Alan fumbled for the right words, but obviously got them close enough for Arthur to understand. Arthur bowed to Mrs. Packer.

To everyone's surprise, Mrs. Packer blushed and curtsied. "It's nice to meet you," she said. "I'm a big fan of your . . . er, legends."

Arthur smiled when Alan translated.

"Would you like his autograph, Mrs. Packer?" Elizabeth said.

The housekeeper shot her an unappreciative look.

Malcolm cleared his throat. "Mrs. Packer, I wanted you to see him so you can go downtown and find him some less-conspicuous clothes. I don't think it's a good idea for him to wander around in his royal vestments. Do you want a measuring tape?"

Mrs. Packer was all business again and quickly sized Arthur up. "Not needed. I'll remember." She left on her errand.

"All right, I think it's time Your Highness and I had a talk," Malcolm said. Through Alan he indicated that they should all sit down. "For one thing, what are you doing here?"

"I do not know," Arthur replied, with Alan translating. "I have said from where I come. I know no more. It may be a dream, a cruel joke, or a trick of Merlin's. I do not know which."

Malcolm, remembering all he had read earlier in the day, decided to test Arthur. "How could this be a trick of Merlin's when he's disappeared? You haven't seen him in years."

Arthur frowned. "Not in the flesh, no. But I have seen the old wizard sometimes in my dreams."

"Tell me about your beautiful sword," Malcolm said.

Arthur instinctively put his hand on the hilt. "Everyone in the kingdom knows of this sword. It is *Excalibur*."

"It must be the one you drew from the stone when you were young," Malcolm said, again testing the man.

Arthur laughed scornfully. "Fie on you, knave. Excalibur was not in the stone—it was given to me by the Lady of the Lake!"

"Please, tell me the story?" Malcolm asked.

"I once fought a tournament with King Pellinore and was wounded," Arthur began. "Merlin took me to a hermit who bound my wounds and gave me good salves to aid their healing. When I was mended, Merlin and I departed. As we rode into a deep wood, I realized that I had no sword. Merlin said it was of no consequence, for a greater sword was soon to be mine. Eventually we came to a lake, and in the middle I saw an arm clothed in white silk reaching heavenward from the water. In its hand was a sword of surpassing beauty. I was dazzled. Then I saw a young woman on the lake, and she came to me and said that the sword would be mine if I gave her whatever gift she asked for. She directed me to take a nearby boat and row to the sword. I rowed to the place and took the sword by the handle. As I marveled at the weapon and tested its feel, the arm and hand swiftly drew under the water again, leaving barely a ripple. I took Excalibur, for so was the sword named, and returned to land."

"He's kidding, right?" Elizabeth said to Jeff.

Jeff shook his head. "Not if the books are true."

"I'd like to hear the story of how you died," Malcolm said to Arthur, knowing this would make or break his theory.

His request led to a brief and angry exchange between Arthur and Alan. Finally Alan turned to Malcolm. "He resents this interrogation. Who are you to riddle him with questions? How dare you ask him about death?"

"He knows how he died?" Malcolm asked.

"No," Alan answered. "That's why he's so mad. He *hasn't* died. He wants to know if this is some kind of trick or dream or premonition about his battle against Mordred."

Malcolm looked thoughtful. "Well, that's interesting."

"What?" Jeff asked.

"Assuming once again that this man isn't some kind of lunatic and is King Arthur, then we've confirmed one thing. He really did slip through time somehow *before* his last battle with Mordred."

"That's what he's been saying all along," Alan stated.

"Are you going to tell him how he dies?" Jeff asked.

"No," Malcolm replied. "Alan, please tell His Majesty that I'm terribly sorry for asking him so many questions. But just as his appearance here is confusing to him, it's equally confusing to us. This isn't a trick, a dream, or a premonition."

Alan translated the message and Arthur responded.

"What did he say?" Malcolm asked.

"He said that he's very hungry." Alan smiled.

Malcolm stood up. "Then let's go raid the kitchen."

Arthur poked, prodded, and smelled the multiple plates of meat, fruits, and vegetables Malcolm put before him. Eventually he dared a taste and, satisfied that it wouldn't harm him, attacked the food with his bare hands.

"That's disgusting," Elizabeth said.

"At least he's authentic," Alan grinned. "Forks weren't commonly used in Europe until a thousand years after Arthur's reign."

"Okay, Uncle Malcolm, what are you thinking?" Jeff asked.

Malcolm had been leaning against the kitchen counter, arms folded, his gaze on no fixed point in that room or even that dimension. "This is a mess."

"You're telling me," Elizabeth said, still watching the indelicate way Arthur tore into the food.

"I'm talking about this situation," Malcolm clarified. "We're at that clichéd fork in the road."

"You're going to have to explain," Alan said.

Malcolm moved away from the counter and slowly paced from one end of the kitchen to the other. "Let's say that he *is* Arthur. What's he doing here?"

"He doesn't seem to know," Alan answered.

"That's the problem," Malcolm said. "If he doesn't know, then how are we supposed to know?"

Jeff snagged a piece of ham. "You're assuming that he's here for a reason. Maybe he's just here because . . . I don't know . . . time hiccuped and brought him here by accident."

"You should know better than anyone that things don't happen simply by accident." Malcolm eyed both Jeff and Elizabeth, and they looked at each other self-consciously. "I don't believe in accidents or coincidences. They're always part of a bigger plan."

Alan nodded silently in affirmation.

Malcolm paced more vigorously. Arthur stopped eating to watch him. "I've been thinking a lot about Fawlt Line. Has anyone ever asked why it's called that?"

"Named after Thaddeus Fawlt back in 1780," Alan offered.

"That's what I always heard, too," Malcolm said. "But I've been studying the history of our town, and there's more to it than that. The town was originally called *Fault* Line, until Thaddeus

Fawlt came along and changed the spelling to suit his name. So why *Fault* Line? It's not as though we're on any kind of geographical fault here."

Arthur said something to Alan.

"He wants to know what you're talking about," Alan reported.

"Yes, Uncle Malcolm, what are you getting at?" Elizabeth asked.

Malcolm shoved his hands into his pockets. "I'm saying that I believe Fawlt Line is on some kind of time fault. That's why things are so strange around here. In fact, things have *always* been strange here. It's just that no one's taken the time to look over our whole history and make the connections."

Everyone stared at him.

Malcolm looked at Jeff and Elizabeth again. "Your adventure made me take the time. We've got over 200 years of random incidents that, when looked at individually, can be easily dismissed. But when you put them all together . . ." He spread his hands and blew out his cheeks. "It's very strange."

Alan coughed uncomfortably. "Do you really want me to say all that to Arthur?"

"Yes," Malcolm said. "It might help him to understand. If we're on some kind of time fault, then it's possible that he slipped through for some reason."

"He's going to want to know how he slipped through and for what reason," Alan guessed.

"I don't know," Malcolm said impatiently. "I'm still trying to figure it out."

Alan began an animated conversation with Arthur.

"Uncle Malcolm," Jeff said thoughtfully. "You said this was a fork in the road. What's the other side of the fork?"

Malcolm gazed intensely at Arthur. "The other side is: this man is out of his mind, and we're at great risk being near him."

At that moment, Alan finished his explanation. Arthur looked in wide-eyed disbelief at Malcolm, then threw his head back and laughed loudly for a long time.

"What next?" Graham Peters said to his wife at the kitchen table. He put his teacup down and looked closer at the small article buried in the center of the London *Herald*.

"What is it?" Anne Peters asked, sitting down at the table and crunching a bite of freshly made toast.

"Apparently there's a man in America who thinks he's King Arthur," Graham said. "He showed up in a field dressed in a cape, tunic, and tights, speaking Latin and swinging a large sword."

Anne giggled. "What would Arthur be doing in America?"

"Sightseeing, I suppose. He was found in a small town somewhere in Maryland." Graham carefully tore out the article.

"What are you doing with it?" Anne asked.

Her husband smiled. "I want to show it to Myrddin. You know how he is about King Arthur."

"Better not show him, Graham," Anne teased. "He'll want to borrow money for a plane ticket."

"Borrow from whom? I'm just his vicar, not the Prince of Wales." He tucked the article into his shirt pocket. "And I may not be his vicar for long."

"Oh, Graham, do stop."

The phone chirped from the front hall, and Anne went to answer it.

The wooden chair creaked as Graham sat back and looked out the kitchen window. He gazed at his church—Christ Church of Wellsbridge—an assemblage of thick and uneven sandstone, sloped Gothic roofs, Roman arches of varying sizes that framed the doorways and tall stained-glass windows, a rose window on the transept, and a square hundred-foot high tower with an elegantly spired crown. As best as anyone could tell, the church was nine hundred years old, perhaps older. But in its long history, it had been through several renovations and restructurings. The oldest part of the church, including the original nave and apse, had recently been cleared away and sent to a buyer in America. *Typical,* Graham had thought at the time. *The Americans appreciate the value of things we've forgotten.*

The people of Wellsbridge certainly didn't value the church. Now it was a neglected monument in need of restoration again. The foundation had slid and settled, leaving the building slumped and in danger of condemnation from building inspectors. But this time there wouldn't be a wealthy patron to rescue it. Just the opposite, in fact. The only wealthy patron in the area was dying to tear the building down and put in its place a "Superstore"—like the American-style warehouse and factory outlets that had recently begun to spring up all over the landscape of England.

Graham sighed. Christ Church of Wellsbridge was ever steadfast, ever faithful, waiting diligently to receive, whether anyone ever came inside its doors or not. Unfortunately, few people did. Wellsbridge didn't have the population to sustain a church. It was the kind of tiny village tourists pictured on a postcard of England but never made their way to see in person. The High Street had a bank, a news agent, a locally owned grocery shop, and The Rose & The Crown Pub. A small road off the High Street led to the rectory, Graham's home for the past three years and, of course, to Christ Church. What else was there? A few small cottages and outlying farms. It was just as easy to go north to the cathedral in Wells or south to a church in Glastonbury.

Which is precisely why so many people thought the church should be closed and a Superstore built in its place. Good for local economy, they kept saying in the village meetings. How could Graham effectively argue against it?

Anne appeared in the doorway. "That was the archdeacon on the phone. He wants to see you right away."

Graham gulped. The archdeacon was the bishop's hatchetman, called upon when there were problems in the parish that the Bishop didn't want to deal with. "What have I done now?"

"He didn't say. He asked me to come as well, but I don't dare miss my luncheon with Mrs. Hammond. It'd be the third week in a row, and she'd never forgive me."

Graham was aghast. "You told the archdeacon you couldn't come with me because of lunch with Mrs. Hammond?"

"Not in so many words." Anne smiled. "But I wouldn't keep him waiting if I were you."

"Sit down, sit down." Neville Vail, the Archdeacon, gestured to Graham from behind his enormous oak desk.

Graham obeyed, sitting nervously on the edge of a gaudy velvet Georgian chair with ornate armrests.

"Tea?"

Graham shook his head. "No, thank you." He wriggled in the chair. Obviously it was designed for looks, not comfort.

"I've called you in to talk about Adrian," the archdeacon said.

"Adrian?" Graham was puzzled. "As in my *son* Adrian?"

"Precisely," the archdeacon said, his bushy eyebrows settling like dark clouds over his eyes.

"What about him?"

"Mostly about the embarrassment he's causing you," the archdeacon said.

Graham's face lit up with surprise.

The archdeacon seemed pleased by Graham's shock and continued. "You will be phoned this afternoon by the headmaster at the Winchester School for Boys. Adrian has been suspended."

"Suspended!" Graham croaked. "For what?"

"Poor test results and insubordinate behavior."

Graham looked blank. He opened his mouth, but he didn't know what to say.

"He doesn't study, and he refuses to obey those in authority over him," the archdeacon explained. "Neither point should surprise you, Graham. You've known how awful his test results have been, and as for not obeying—well, there's little left to be said about that. Would you like to see the headmaster's report? He faxed it to me first thing this morning."

Graham shook his head in disbelief. "I don't understand.

Adrian simply isn't like this."

"Nonsense," the archdeacon snapped. "He's been a source of consternation for you for as long as I've known you."

"Since I became vicar of Christ Church," Graham said softly.

"The point is: what are you going to do about him?"

Graham was dazed. He didn't have the slightest idea what to do. He had been certain that Adrian's attitude problems and constant mischief-making were the result of the move to Wellsbridge. Prior to that, Graham had been the vicar of a church in the urban center of Bristol and, though he and Adrian had the usual father and teenage son squabbles, things had been all right between them. Graham's assignment to the church in Wellsbridge and the relatively quiet lifestyle there changed all that. Adrian became restless and belligerent. He made friends with a few local boys who despised everything Graham and Anne held dear. He blatantly disregarded curfew and often came home drunk, either alone or taxied by the police. Arguments between father and son turned into red-faced shouting matches.

The breaking point had come with the church tower incident. Adrian and his friends had a contest to see who could throw their empty beer bottles the furthest from the top of the church. Adrian scored the highest by not only throwing a bottle far enough to reach the street, but by hitting a passing car. A police car.

Graham and Anne decided to send him to school in Winchester, where they hoped he would get out from under the influence of his friends and the boredom of the area. It seemed they had hoped for too much.

Blast this chair. Graham wriggled again. "With all due respect, Neville," he said, "why are *you* telling me about this? Why didn't the headmaster call me directly?"

"The headmaster and I are old schoolmates, and he thought that something this sensitive should be passed on for my consideration," the archdeacon answered.

"How thoughtful of him."

"Look, Graham, you know how people feel about the vicar

and his family. They're to be above reproach. Do I have to invoke the numerous biblical passages on the subject?"

Graham hung his head and didn't answer.

"It's expected that a vicar's house should be kept in order, his family under control."

"At heart he's a good lad," Graham began, then stopped. It sounded like a poor excuse.

"His goodheartedness isn't helping his behavior much," the archdeacon said curtly.

Graham spread his hands in appeal. "I don't know what to do. His mother and I have tried to instill goodness and faith in him, but he doesn't buy it. Like most boys his age, he doesn't seem to believe in anything at all."

"You'll have to try harder," the archdeacon warned, then added for good measure, "The bishop isn't pleased."

"The bishop?" Graham asked helplessly, wondering, *Am I the last person in the church hierarchy to know about my son's dismissal?*

"I don't have to tell you how this sort of thing can affect your career. I've seen priests headed for the bishopric suddenly knocked out by a rebellious child. It doesn't look good. It doesn't look good at all."

Graham shifted in the chair once again.

The archdeacon continued, "And it certainly doesn't help the future of Christ Church."

Graham had been waiting for that statement.

"As you know, we've been discussing this for several months now. Richard Ponsonby has made an offer to the bishop for the church, the rectory, and surrounding acreage. If he is successful . . ." The archdeacon let the rest of the sentence go unspoken. Graham knew what the silence meant. Chances were, if he lost Christ Church, he wouldn't be moved to another. His career was on the precipice. And his son was helping to push him over.

"I don't believe there's anything more to say," the archdeacon announced with a slap of both palms on the desktop. He made as if to stand, but didn't. Graham did. "Your son will be arriving at the Wells Train Station on the 11:50."

Adrian squeezed his luggage into the back of the mini, then sat down silently in the passenger seat. At fifteen years of age, he was still in an awkward growth stage, and his legs didn't seem to know where to go in the small car. Graham pulled away from the front of the train station and into the noonday traffic. It was early for the tourist season, but Wells was unusually congested.

"So?" Graham asked when they had cleared town and were on the A39 headed for Wellsbridge.

"So?"

"I think an explanation of some sort is in order."

"Like what?"

"You're creative, think of something."

Adrian scratched his chin. "How about: the teachers and students didn't like me, so I was the scapegoat for everything that went wrong."

"Is that true?"

"No."

"Then try again."

"Everyone had that typical upper-class priggish snobbery. I didn't fit in."

"Is that true?" Graham asked again.

"No."

"Then—"

"Look, Dad, nothing's true except that I hated it there and I couldn't be bothered to get along, all right? That's it. Full stop." Adrian slumped down into his seat and bit at a fingernail.

"Well, that's just grand, isn't it?" Graham said with clenched anger. "You couldn't be bothered. All that money spent on your private school fees, and you couldn't be bothered. Your mother spending night after sleepless night worrying about you, and you couldn't be bothered. My reputation as a vicar going down the drain, and you couldn't be bothered. Then, by all means, tell me what might motivate you to be bothered?"

"Not much," Adrian said.

"I beg your pardon?"

Adrian folded his arms. "Not much. I mean, what's the point?"

"What's the point? Is that what you just said?" Graham suddenly shouted. "The point is that you need to straighten yourself out, that's the point! I'm a vicar, and your antics could very well cost me my job!"

Adrian didn't say anything for a moment. Then he spoke so softly that Graham almost missed it. "So?" Adrian asked.

"So!" Graham nearly lost control of the car.

Adrian didn't speak.

"Is that what this is all about? You've been thrown out of school to come home and tell me that there's no point to my job?" Graham asked.

"I was thinking about it the other day and, well, it's not as if you enjoy what you do," Adrian said calmly. "Wellsbridge is the end of the earth, after all. So maybe it's time you got a new job."

"Get your head out of the clouds, Adrian. Enjoyment has nothing to do with it. I'm *called* to my job. That's what being a vicar is. A calling. And if it takes me to places like Wellsbridge, then that's God's business."

"Yeah, right," Adrian said. "The bishop's business, you mean."

Graham tried to remember when and why he had stopped spanking Adrian. He was tempted to pull the car over and reacquaint them both with the experience. He prayed for patience. "This conversation has nothing to do with the problem at hand, Adrian."

"Doesn't it?"

"No, because *you're* the problem at hand. We should be talking about you." Graham's voice grew more intense. "Why do you persist in getting into trouble? I don't understand what's going on in that muddled brain of yours. You're fifteen years old, yet you act like you're ten. No, I take that back. You were a good boy at ten. You were a good boy even up to thirteen. But in the last two years, it's as if we don't know you! All you do is make our lives miserable. What happened to that nice young man we once knew? You used to be so kind and responsible—a good Christian boy, a boy any vicar would be proud to have as a son. *What happened?*"

Adrian bit at another nail. "I asked myself: what's the point? And I couldn't come up with any answers."

"You're joking. That's all you have to say?"

"Near enough," Adrian said. "What's the point? I'm asking you sincerely. What's the point whether or not I do well in school? What's the point whether you're vicar of Christ Church in Wellsbridge? What's the point of anything?"

"You're a philosopher now, is that it?"

Adrian sat up suddenly. "I'm serious, Dad. You want to know what my problem is? It's that I don't see a flippin' point to anything we do!"

The passion of Adrian's statement caused Graham to pause for a moment. His son was in a spiritual crisis, and he hadn't even realized it. "The point is . . ." Graham began carefully. "The point is that we're here to . . . we need to find our place in this world and . . . to serve God . . . and to love our neighbors and . . ." Graham's answer was so lacking in conviction that he couldn't finish it.

"See? *You* don't even know," Adrian said. "When was the last time you believed anything you were doing? It's a joke. You're a career priest. You don't believe there's a point any more than I do!"

His son's words stung Graham at the most tender part of his heart. Was he a career priest—worried mostly about his position in the church—or was he there to serve God in whatever capacity God chose? In his younger days as a believer and later as a new priest, there was no question in his mind. He was part of God's work here on earth. To love God with all his heart, soul, mind, and body. To love his neighbor as himself. It invigorated him, drove him with a sense of vision even in the worst of times. Meetings with bishops and archdeacons and even the powerfully rich didn't faze him. But now . . .

Now?

What do I believe?

CHAPTER 9

"I think he's looking older," Malcolm observed to Alan. They were looking out from the French doors in Malcolm's study at Arthur. He was dressed in the modern clothes that Mrs. Packer bought for him, walking around the garden, hands clasped behind his back and head hung low. He'd been with them for a full day now, and in that short time his hair had gone grayer and the lines on his face deeper.

"I agree," Alan said. "But what can we do for him?"

Malcolm turned away from windows, his brow furrowed. "I wish I knew."

"Do you believe he's King Arthur?" Alan asked.

Malcolm looked at Alan thoughtfully, then nodded. "Yes. Do you?"

"If he isn't, then he's a remarkable fraud," Alan said. "I thought I knew Latin well, but he uses words in an authentic context—in a way that couldn't have been picked up from a textbook. It *sounds* right."

Malcolm smiled at him, the obvious question forthcoming.

Alan waved it away. "Don't ask me how or why he's here in our time. I haven't the slightest idea. But I've seen enough around this town to believe that the impossible is possible and that there's usually a reason behind it. He's here—and we have to help him."

Questions hung in the air between them. How could they help? What could they do for a man who had slipped through time for reasons he didn't even know? What was his mission? What part did they play in it?

"I think it's disgraceful," Mrs. Packer said as she entered with a tray of tea.

"Disgraceful?" Malcolm asked.

"All this hand-wringing and worrying. It's perfectly obvious what you have to do." She put the tray on the table with a noticeable rattle of cups.

"We're on pins and needles, Mrs. Packer," Malcolm said.

"First, you need to pray very hard," she said.

"A given," Alan acknowledged.

"And then you need to get him to England."

Malcolm and Alan looked at her quizzically.

She put her hands on her hips impatiently. "I've told you what my grandmother said. If Arthur is back, then he's come back to help Britain in its greatest time of need."

"How is this Britain's greatest time of need?" Malcolm inquired.

"Oh, questions, questions, and more questions!" Mrs. Packer cried out. "You're the one who goes on and on about faith. Why don't you show a little faith and take some action? Getting him to Britain makes a lot more sense than standing around here waiting for something to happen!"

Just then the French doors opened, and Arthur stepped in. Through Alan he said, "Take me to the church."

"The church? Why?" Malcolm asked.

"To pray!" he answered.

Arthur kept his eyes closed as they drove him to the church in the jeep. "I do not like this chariot!" he shouted over the wind and the roar of the motor. When they arrived, he got out on wobbly legs and said that it was against nature for a chariot to move without the aid of horses.

"It has horses," Malcolm laughed, "but they're under the hood."

Inside the dark ruin, Arthur went to the stone table, crossed himself, and knelt down.

Malcolm and Alan looked at each other, shrugged, and also knelt to pray.

Half an hour later, Arthur crossed himself again and stood up. He turned to face Malcolm and Alan and announced that he could bear it no longer.

"Bear what?" Malcolm asked.

"This waiting and doing nothing!" he said through his translator. "While I wear these strange clothes, pace in your gardens, and am entertained by your enchantments, Mordred is stealing my kingdom!"

Malcolm held up his hand. "I have a theory about that, Your Highness. If Mordred took over your kingdom, then all of history would change, since he didn't succeed originally."

Arthur cocked an eyebrow. "Didn't he, by God? Are you saying that he was defeated in our battle?"

Malcolm chose his words carefully. "I can honestly say that, yes, he was defeated. But it would be wrong to say anything else."

"Pray what is your theory, sir?" Arthur asked.

"Since history *hasn't* changed, then I can only assume that Mordred hasn't taken over your kingdom. I suspect that your time has been frozen by your absence and will resume when you return."

"That sounds ridiculous," Alan said before he translated what Malcolm had said.

Malcolm shrugged. "So is his being here. But he is, and I can only assume that somehow time fractured or bent in order for it to happen. Maybe the hours he spends with us will only seem like seconds in his time."

Alan smiled. "It sounds impressive, even if it's wrong." He translated the message to Arthur.

Arthur shook his head, bewildered. "I do not understand how this can be, yet I hope you are right. For if Mordred takes my kingdom, all is lost. He is a brutally cruel man. He tortures the helpless for sport. He is without a knight's virtue or a nobleman's honor. He is an evil shadow on the face of my land." Arthur pounded his fist on the stone slab. "I must serve my purpose here and go home!"

Malcolm tugged at his ear with a resolute look in his eyes. "Then let's get you to England so you can do both."

CHAPTER 10

As an initial punishment for getting thrown out of school, Graham made Adrian help him with his work around Christ Church. They spent the afternoon cutting the grass and clearing away the weeds from the stone sidewalk and along the side of the church. Afterwards, with a shovel, pick, and wheelbarrow, they trudged around to the south side of the church where the oldest section had once stood. Parts of the ruin still remained, but mostly as random piles of stones.

"Crumbs!" Adrian exclaimed. "This looks different."

Graham agreed. After the ruins had been carted off to America, he had begun to tear the ground up with a tiller. "I want to plant another garden here," he told Adrian. "Maybe I'll put in a couple of benches and make this a garden for meditation."

Adrian leaned against the shovel handle, now sticking up out of the dirt. "Some American really paid money for that old wreck of a building? Who was he, someone with more dollars than sense?"

"The archdeacon worked out the details," Graham said as he thrust his shovel into the dirt and began to dig. "I only met him for a moment. He was some sort of history enthusiast. He wants to build a village dedicated to time."

"Like St. Fagan's," Adrian said. "It's a village outside Cardiff that has farmhouses and shops and schools, all from different periods of history. I went there on a school trip. Remember?"

Graham didn't. "Are you going to stand there and talk or are you going to help me?"

"Do I have a choice?"

"No."

"Then I think I'll help you." Adrian pulled his shovel out of the ground and joined his father digging.

Graham noticed several chunks of stone littering the ground along the church wall. He peered up where they came from and saw cracks and holes near the edge of the roof. More evidence of the building's subsidence, he knew.

"What's that?" Adrian asked.

"Debris," Graham said and returned to his digging. "The church's foundation is sinking."

"Isn't that dangerous?"

Graham nodded. "It's not dangerous to the congregation, but it's dangerous to me. If the building inspectors find out before I can get the money to restore it, they'll close the church."

"How much money do you have so far?"

"Not a penny," Graham said helplessly.

"Then why bother?" Adrian asked. "It's not as if it has any value. You have three blue-haired old ladies who attend services regularly, plus the occasional walking tourists who get lost. And Myrddin, who most people think is mad."

"That's not the point," Graham said.

Adrian acted as if he hadn't heard. "The church doesn't even have any important history connected to it. What does it have? That bizarre stone altar, and that's about all."

The stone altar at the head of the church was carved ornately from solid Somerset rock. One historian guessed from the design that it might have been done as early as the fifth century.

"That altar must be worth a lot of money. The archdeacon didn't let it go to the American."

"No, he sent the stone priest's table instead. He wants the altar for the museum in Wells," Graham explained.

"There you are, then," Adrian said. "You could lose this church and no one would notice."

Graham felt deflated. "Thank you, son. I appreciate your support."

Graham and Adrian dug silently for a moment. Graham lost himself in the depressing situation that stood before him. How could he solicit funds for the restoration of the church without drawing undue attention to the church's condition? For he had no doubt that once the word got out, Richard Ponsonby would make his move to close Christ Church down and secure the land for his Superstore.

As if on cue, Ponsonby himself rolled in like an unexpected storm and was upon Graham before the vicar had a chance to duck for cover—his general feeling whenever Ponsonby was around. Check your wallet and head for the hills.

Ponsonby was a wealthy and powerful man who had taken his family's modest inherited wealth and, through ruthless dealings, turned it into a fortune. British diplomacy and gentlemanly fair practice were not part of his conduct. He was one of the new breed of merciless businessmen who did whatever was necessary to fulfill their ambitions—and heaven help whoever got in the way.

"Look who's here!" Anne declared with artificial brightness as she rounded the corner of the church. She looked at Graham with an apologetic expression, then quickly left again.

"Our beloved vicar in backbreaking labor!" Ponsonby said heartily as he continued toward them, dressed smartly in tailored trousers and complementary sport jacket. "And people say our church leaders are never down to earth. What a testimony!"

"Hello, Mr. Ponsonby," Graham said. He tossed a shovelful of dirt onto the chunks of stone that had fallen from the wall. Ponsonby was the last person on earth who should see those.

"Adrian, you're back from school." Ponsonby smiled at the boy, who nodded silently.

Graham had no doubt that Ponsonby knew everything there was to know about Adrian's dismissal. For an instant, he felt renewed anger at his son for giving Ponsonby one more failure to lord over him.

"I see your father has wasted no time in putting you to work," Ponsonby said. "Good for him. I'm a big believer in hard work. It was hard work that gave me my first million before I was twenty-seven."

Right, thought Graham. *Other people's hard work.*

Ponsonby turned back to the vicar. "I thought you should know that I put in a new offer to the bishop for this church and lands," he said.

Graham lifted another shovelful of dirt and threw it onto the remaining chunk of stone. "Really. How interesting." *He's riding on the coattails of Adrian's dismissal. It's a perfect time to impress the bishop that the vicar of Christ Church should be removed and the church torn down,* Graham thought.

"You can't blame me," Ponsonby asserted. "It's a terrible misuse of resources for you to spend so much time caring for a church that isn't needed in this area."

"I appreciate your deep concern about the church's resources and my time, Mr. Ponsonby. However, I would respectfully submit that churches are needed in every area. It's more Superstores that aren't needed, I suspect."

Ponsonby chuckled. "Well, now, that's where we'll have to disagree. What do you think, Adrian? Are you for progress or against it?"

Adrian stopped digging. He chose the words for his answer carefully. "Frankly, it doesn't matter to me one way or the other. I'm not sure that a Superstore represents progress any more than I believe that this church represents anything more than wishful thinking from the past."

Ponsonby clapped his hands. "An excellent answer! I believe you've knocked us both with that one. Don't you agree, Graham? In one sentence he blasted both of us."

Graham gazed at his son. "He's good at that."

"You have a bright boy here," Ponsonby continued. "He's quick on his feet."

"Not very quick with that shovel, though," Graham said.

"Ho, ho. Are you going to look for a job now that you're out of school, Adrian?"

Adrian shrugged. "I don't know."

"I'd be pleased if you'd come to see me. I could use someone like you on my estate. That is, if your father wouldn't mind." He turned to Graham. "You wouldn't be threatened if your son came to see me, would you, Graham?"

Graham clenched the shovel handle and stabbed it into the thick earth. "Threatened? Why would that threaten me?"

"Excellent!" Ponsonby said. "Then you don't mind. Good. Come and visit me, Adrian, and we'll see what we can do for you."

"Thanks. Maybe I will."

"Or maybe you won't," Graham muttered. "Adrian is out of school for the moment," he said to Ponsonby, "but that doesn't mean he'll stay out of school."

Ponsonby scoffed, "Oh, school. Overrated, I reckon. School never helped me in any of my business. It's what you have instinctively up here." He tapped the side of his head. "That's what matters."

"Perhaps that worked for you, but I doubt if—"

Ponsonby cut Graham off. "I just want to talk to him, Graham. I want to see what he's made of. It certainly won't do him any harm. All things considered, it might do him a world of good."

There was something about the way he said "all things considered" that made Graham want to attack Ponsonby with his shovel. "All things considered" meant "Considering what a rotten job you've done with your son." But Graham imagined the headlines in the tabloid newspapers—VICAR ATTACKS RICH CHURCH MEMBER WITH SHOVEL—and thought better of it.

"Why not, Dad? You don't want me hanging around here bored all day, do you? You know what boredom does to me."

Graham suddenly felt that he was being manipulated by two wills much stronger than his own. Ponsonby had one agenda, Adrian another. They were pushing all the right buttons to get the desired responses. If he were a more forceful father or a more astute pastor he would have been able to say just the right thing to assert his control—to show them both who was really in charge of this situation. But standing there with a sweat-soaked handkerchief tied around his head and a shovel poised in his trembling hands, he didn't feel like the boss. He felt like a broken-down church whose foundations were subsiding. Useless, tired, and slumped.

"It's up to you, son," Graham finally answered.

CHAPTER 11

"Myrddin?" Graham called as he tapped on the splintered wooden door.

From somewhere inside the old ramshackle cottage he heard his friend call out. "Hullo, Graham. Come in. I've made you some tea."

Graham opened the door and stepped in. "You have? But how did you know I was coming? I didn't know myself until a few minutes ago."

"Sit down, sit down," Myrddin said impatiently. "We have much to talk about."

Myrddin was in the tiny kitchen, separated from the main room by a counter. The teapot rattled and water splashed. Graham sat down in a thick oak chair that might've been a couple of hundred years old. He didn't know its age any more than he knew Myrddin's. It was timeless, like Myrddin himself. From where he sat, he could see Myrddin's head bobbing up and down as he prepared the tray of tea. His wild white hair danced around like a loose halo. His robe hung on him like a monk's habit on a skeleton.

With thin shaking hands, Myrddin put the tray on a small table that did double duty as a server and a desk. "Things are happening, Graham," he said, a thin smile stretching across his bony face. His cheeks were flushed, and his blue eyes were childlike in their alertness.

It was Myrddin's eyes that impressed Graham more than anything; though the old man's angular, skeletal body and waxed-paper skin made him look like a walking corpse, his eyes betrayed a soul that was quickened, certainly more alive than many people much younger.

Myrddin leaned forward across the table and said again, "Things are happening!"

Graham poured the tea and said sadly, "They certainly are. My church is about to be declared a safety hazard."

Myrddin waved the comment away. "Minor repairs. I'm talking about—"

"Not minor, Myrddin," Graham interrupted. "It's worse than you think. The foundation is sinking. If Ponsonby finds out just how badly the church is damaged, he'll have his Superstore in no time at all. It's awful. And I haven't told you about Adrian. He was thrown out of school. And I heard about it from the archdeacon."

"Yes, yes, of course. But I'm talking something more important than that," Myrddin said.

Graham frowned. "I'm sorry, but my church and my family are falling apart, and I'll likely be out of a job by this time next year. I fail to see what could be more important."

"How about a miracle, eh? How about something that will change how we look at the world?" Myrddin had *that* look in his eyes. In three years, Graham had come to know that look well. It meant that the old man was up to something.

"What are you talking about?" Graham asked, not sure he wanted to hear.

Myrddin dramatically held up a bony finger. It looked like an exclamation mark. "The return of Arthur!" he announced.

Graham stirred his tea. "Oh, you've seen the newspaper, then."

"Newspaper? No, I haven't. What about it?"

Graham fished in his shirt pocket for the article he had torn out of the paper earlier, and was disappointed to find it wasn't there. "Oh, bother. I put on a clean shirt after working at the church. I must've left the clipping in the other pocket. It said that a man claiming to be King Arthur showed up in some small town in America. I thought you'd be interested. Sorry, I forgot."

"When? When did he show up?" Myrddin asked.

Graham sipped his tea. "A couple of days ago."

Myrddin clasped his hands in childlike delight. "I knew it!"

"Calm down, old man," Graham said.

"But, Graham—"

"Anne told me not to mention it to you. She said you would get yourself in a state."

"You don't think this is worth getting in a state over?" Myrddin exclaimed. "King Arthur returned. It's perfect, absolutely perfect!"

Graham was chagrined. "I don't see what's so perfect about it. He's in America."

"A slight inconvenience, I'm sure." Myrddin scratched at his scruffy beard as he paced around the room. He was lost in his own thoughts. "The time was right. I knew it. I could feel it. I wonder what his plan is. I wonder how he'll get here."

"I doubt he'll get anywhere. Don't Americans lock up crazy people?"

Myrddin frowned. "Do they?"

"Probably," Graham said. "You wouldn't stand a chance, you old fool. One look at you, and they'd have you in a padded room."

"Do you think I'm crazy?" Myrddin asked in earnest.

Graham smiled with undisguised affection. "I think you're pathetic. Now draw deep into your well of wisdom and tell me what I'm going to do about Ponsonby and my church."

"Do you know what I think?" Myrddin asked. "I think you should forget about him. Our horizons just got bigger. Bigger than Ponsonby and Christ Church . . . even bigger than your problems with Adrian."

"Because King Arthur is coming back," Graham groaned. "Sometimes I think I'd feel terribly sorry for you if I didn't consider you such a good friend."

"You think I'm a lunatic. What makes me such a good friend?"

Graham shrugged. "You make a good cup of tea."

CHAPTER 12

Ponsonby Manor was a sprawling, gray eighteenth-century manor house, allegedly built for Robert Ponsonby by King George III as an expression of gratitude. Why the king said thank you to Robert Ponsonby in such a grandiose way was not known. People at the time speculated that it had something to do with questionable business dealings done on His Majesty's behalf.

A stiff servant, with a face as gray as the stone entrance, greeted Adrian Peters at the door and quietly led him to the "study." *This room is as big as our entire house*, Adrian thought as he sat down in a plush wingback chair. The room had everything Adrian expected a rich man's study to have. Dark cherry wood paneling with ornately carved bookshelves stuffed with carefully arranged leather binders, a desk the size of a small van, antique furniture tastefully displayed on several Persian carpets, tapestries, the obligatory globe of the world, a large fireplace topped with two very long crossed swords under a family crest, and huge windows with warped glass, distorting the outside world.

"I'm glad you came to see me, Adrian," Ponsonby said as he strode into the room. He shook Adrian's hand vigorously. "It shows ambition on your part."

Adrian shrugged. "It was either this or stay home and watch the telly with Mum and Dad."

Ponsonby laughed as he circled his enormous desk and settled in his burgundy leather chair. "You're a bright lad."

Adrian smiled politely. "Look, Mr. Ponsonby, I appreciate the offer of a job, but I think—"

"Did I offer you a job? I thought I asked you to come see me about one. But I don't remember making an offer." Ponsonby gave Adrian a coy look.

"Sorry. You're right." Adrian flushed. "But before we go any—"

"I understand that you like cars," Ponsonby interrupted.

"I work on them when I get a chance."

"I'm in need of someone to take care of my cars. I have a few that I'm particularly fond of. Do you want to see them?" Ponsonby was on his feet again.

"If you want me to."

"No, Adrian," Ponsonby corrected him. "Say yes because *you* want to. We won't get anywhere if you play it limp-wristed with me. Reminds me of someone else we both know. Now, do you want to see my cars or not?"

Adrian was so surprised by the sudden rebuke that he could barely mumble, "Yes, sir."

"That's better. Follow me."

They walked silently from the study, back down the hall into the large foyer, and out through the front door. Crossing the cobblestone semicircular driveway, they approached a long building that looked like a stable. The ten square doors on the front betrayed its conversion to a garage. They stepped though a pedestrian door within one of the larger doors, and Adrian's eyes grew wide at the sight before him. A row of beautiful cars sat in regal sophistication under fluorescent lights.

Ponsonby gestured to each one as they walked past. "This red one is a Ferrari 410 Super America. Only five in the country. This, in British racing green, is an E-type Jaguar, V-12 model. This beauty is my Rolls Royce Silver Ghost. I believe you'll recognize my Aston-Martin DB-4. And in a specially created navy blue shade, my Bristol Beaufighter. It's hand built."

"Crumbs!" was all Adrian could manage to say. "These are all yours?"

Ponsonby nodded. "I'm not one for driving cars myself. But I love to look at them. And they certainly make an impression on visitors."

"I'm sure they do," Adrian croaked. His mouth had gone dry.

"Do you know why I bought these cars?" Ponsonby asked.

"Why?"

"Because I could afford to. When I put down cash for a car like, say, that Ferrari, without feeling so much as a pinch or a tingle of concern that there'll be enough left over for other things, it reminds me of who I am. It reminds me that I've reached a point in my life when I can have what I want when I want it. Do you know what that feels like?"

"No, sir."

Ponsonby lips curled into a cruel smile. "Of course you don't. And you never will, as long as you persist in being a failure."

Adrian felt as though Ponsonby had slapped him in the face. *What does this guy want from me, anyway?* "Maybe I should leave," he said.

Ponsonby held up a hand. "No. Don't run away. The truth can be cruel, but it should never be ignored. Listen to me, Adrian. There are people who would give their left arms to hear what I'm telling you for free. Don't persist in being a failure."

"I don't understand," Adrian confessed.

"What was that business at school, eh? Bad test results, stupid pranks . . . for what? What will that do for you, for your future? Nothing. When I was your age—no, don't look at me like that—when I was your age, I was working hard and thinking about the future. Why? Because I knew that by the time I reached the age of forty I wanted to be able to walk into my garage and look at cars like these."

"But you were born rich."

"I was born into a rich family," Ponsonby corrected.

"What's the difference?"

Ponsonby turned to face Adrian. "The difference is that my father insisted that each one of his children prove himself. He pitted us against one another to gain favor for the top position in his will when he died. Obviously, I won."

"But I don't think I'd want to base my life on acquiring cars," Adrian said.

"Then don't," Ponsonby replied simply. "But what do you want to base your life on? Make up your mind and then go for it. Take all you can from life, and don't give anything back. Determine your plan. If it includes school, then do your absolute best there. Not because it's what your parents want or because you think it's the right thing to do, but because it suits your plan—because it's the thing *you* want to do. I think you're smarter than you like to let on. I see the fire in your eyes. And do you know what else I see?"

"What?"

"I see myself at your age. You're trying to decide the meaning of life, your purpose, what you believe in. I'm here to help you decide." Ponsonby casually leaned over the rear fender of the Rolls Royce and brushed at a tiny piece of lint.

Adrian was overwhelmed. His brain seemed to be working in slow motion. "Hold on. Why do you want to help me decide?"

"I can't stand waste, Adrian. And I think it would be a waste for you to . . . I shouldn't say it."

"Say what?"

Ponsonby shuffled awkwardly, but it looked contrived. "I think it would be a waste for you to wind up like your father." He exhaled as if a huge weight had been taken from his shoulders. "There. My cards are on the table. I look at you, and I see myself thirty years ago. My heart goes out to you. I want to rescue you."

Adrian felt numb. "Rescue me how?"

"By offering you that job. I want you to help take care of my cars."

"But . . . why me?" Adrian stammered.

"Why not you?"

"Because . . . well, I don't know, really, except . . ."

Ponsonby frowned at him and spoke with irritation in his voice. "Adrian, if you insist on continuing with this imitation of your father, I'll retract the offer and send you home. I'm saying this only once. But, unlike a lot of offers you'll get, you should know now that this one may change the direction of your life. You have the potential to stand in your own garage and look at your own collection of cars—or whatever you fancy. Or you could wind up a good but trampled man trying to save things that aren't worth saving—like that old church of your father's. Which are you going to do?"

The next morning saw King Arthur having his first modern shower, which Mrs. Packer refused to help with, and a trim of his hair and beard, which she was more than happy to provide. "As scruffy as you look, I can't imagine what Guinevere saw in you!" she said as she cut away, knowing he couldn't understand her.

Jeff showed Arthur how to dress in a suit, but gave up on trying to get him to wear a tie.

Malcolm applauded when Arthur made his appearance at the breakfast table. Elizabeth, who had just arrived with her father, looked curiously at Arthur, then at Malcolm. "What's going on here, Uncle Malcolm? Why do you have him dressed up like that?"

Malcolm took a slurpy bite of his grapefruit. "Well, I can't take him to the British Embassy looking like . . . like . . ."

"Like King Arthur," Jeff finished for him.

"Right," Malcolm said.

"The British Embassy!" Elizabeth exclaimed. "You mean, the one in Washington, D.C.?"

"The one and only," Malcolm said. "We can't get him to England without a passport."

Elizabeth watched as Arthur attacked everything on the breakfast table. "Apart from his table manners, he's a pretty good-looking man now that he's cleaned up."

"Particularly when you consider that he's over a thousand years old," Jeff observed.

Alan, lost in his own thoughts for a moment, suddenly asked, "Are you going to drug him?"

"What?" Malcolm responded. "Drug him? Why?"

"You saw how he was in the jeep yesterday. How's he going to react to your plane?"

Arthur shouted at the top of his lungs.

"We should have drugged him," Malcolm admitted as he

guided the twin-engine plane into the skies and south toward Washington.

"Told you so," Alan said, then turned to Arthur. "Your Majesty! Look at me! Fix your eyes on me!"

Arthur stopped shouting and looked wildly at Alan. "How is this possible? How can we fly as the birds fly?"

"It's like all of the other machines you have seen," Alan explained in Latin. "This one allows us to fly."

Arthur looked at him with childlike amazement. "Will you teach me to do it? What a marvel this will be for my people!"

"I don't think that would be a very good idea," Alan said. "Meanwhile, maybe you should just close your eyes and sit back for the rest of the trip. It won't be so frightening that way."

"You dare to say I'm frightened?" Arthur growled menacingly.

"Of course not, Your Majesty." Alan turned forward again and gave Malcolm a knowing look. "He says he's not frightened."

Arthur slowly leaned toward the small round window and peered out. Below him were scattered pillows of clouds and rolling green farmlands.

He gave another shout.

The drive from National Airport gave Arthur an instant education in the hustle and bustle of a city—in this case, the nation's capital. Malcolm purposefully played the tour guide and took him past Washington's most important sites. Arthur's head seemed to turn a complete 360 degrees as he looked and pointed at everything from the crowds of people at the crosswalks to the Greek-style architectural tributes to Lincoln and Jefferson and, of course, the Washington Monument.

The British Passport and Visa Office wasn't part of the British Embassy as Malcolm thought. It was about a hundred yards away, closer to the New Zealand Embassy, on Massachusetts Avenue. It was housed in a nondescript building with a small reception area, and beleaguered visa officers rushed to and fro behind thick security windows. Once Malcolm was able to explain the complexity of the situation to a helpful young woman behind the glass, they were ushered through a large door to a small cubicle. Ian Walters, a balding civil servant who'd been in America long enough to lose some of his British accent, asked all three men to sit down.

Ian was nearly lost behind the stacks of folders and papers on his metal desk. "What can I do for you?" he asked.

Malcolm gestured to Arthur. "He needs a passport to get back to England."

"Oh? Did he lose his?"

Malcolm looked uncomfortably at Alan, then at Ian again. "Well, not exactly."

Ian tapped his pencil on the top of the desk. "Destroyed? Stolen?"

"No. He never really had one."

"He never had a British passport," Ian repeated. "I see. A European passport, then?"

"No."

Ian scratched his cheek and turned to Arthur. "Are you a British subject?"

"Sort of," Malcolm answered for him.

"Can't he speak for himself?" Ian asked suspiciously.

"Not really." Malcolm swallowed hard. "He only speaks Latin."

"Latin."

"Yes, sir."

Ian pushed back from his desk. "I think you may have the wrong office."

"Wait," Malcolm said. "You see, he's a British subject—that is, he's originally from England—but he wound up here by accident and now he needs to go back."

"Can you show me some identification? A birth certificate, driver's license, return plane ticket . . . anything that might prove his citizenship?"

"I'm sorry, I can't."

"If he's been living here in the United States, then he must surely have *something* with which to identify himself. Social security card? Credit card? Library card?" Ian's tone was now sarcastic.

Malcolm shook his head.

"Has he been living under a rock?"

For a moment, Malcolm considered lying—making up a tragic story about a fire that destroyed all of Arthur's possessions and left him with amnesia. He thought better of it and answered with an embarrassed shrug.

"Then I think you're out of luck. We can't just issue a passport to anyone who wants one. Perhaps you should try the American embassy. Or the Italian Embassy, since he speaks Latin. Though I doubt they'll be able to help you without proper identification."

In the hall again, Malcolm sipped some water from the water fountain to help soothe his dry mouth.

"Well," Alan said. "What next?"

Malcolm wiped his mouth. "Pray for a miracle."

Arthur demanded to know what was going on, and Alan explained it to him. Arthur was indignant and wanted to throw Ian in a dungeon for questioning his identity.

Malcolm and Alan were in the middle of explaining why it would be unwise to try and throw Ian into a dungeon when suddenly someone called out Malcolm's name.

All three men spun around. Coming toward them was a young man—no more than thirty—dressed in a loose-fitting suit that made him look like a young bank executive. Malcolm thought his face was vaguely familiar.

"It *is* Malcolm Dubbs, isn't it?" the young man asked in a cultured British accent.

"Yes, it is," Malcolm said.

"Oh, good," he said, relieved. "Now you're trying to work out who *I* am."

"Well—"

"It's all right. I don't expect you to remember me—particularly since I was a barely a teenager last time we met." The young man smiled brightly. "I'm David Jenkins, son of Simon."

Malcolm's face lit up. "No! It's not possible!"

Malcolm had spent a year in England doing research at Oxford for a joint American-British government project. His British counterpart was Simon Jenkins. Malcolm had spent a lot of time at the Jenkins home in nearby Headington.

"I didn't give you permission to grow up."

David laughed casually. "You haven't changed at all." He looked at Alan and Arthur expectantly.

"Oh," Malcolm said, remembering himself. "I'd like you to meet Alan Forde and Arthur . . . er, Arthur Pendragon."

David shook hands with Alan but hesitated when he took Arthur's hand. "Arthur *Pendragon*? Very interesting. A descendent of King Arthur, I assume?" he said with a chuckle.

Arthur stared at him incomprehensibly, and Malcolm and Alan merely glanced away awkwardly.

Malcolm recovered the situation. "David's father and I did some work on a little project for our respective governments together in Oxford."

"Little!" David said to Alan and Arthur. "They spent a whole year locked up in the Bodleian library. We still don't know what they were up to. Top secret, they kept saying. My father was nearly given a knighthood for the work they did."

"How is the old codger?"

"Cantankerous as ever," David said. "He'll be thrilled to hear I've seen you. You two should do more than just exchange Christmas cards. He misses you."

Malcolm smiled. "I think of him often. I keep promising myself to visit him if I ever get back to England. What are you doing here? Wait—I remember now—your father wrote and said you work for you-know-who."

Malcolm was referring to MI5, the department of the British Secret Service.

David nodded. "I'm on temporary assignment to the embassy for reasons I can't explain."

Arthur, obviously impatient with all the chatting, suddenly

asked Alan if this man would help them get to England.

David was surprised. "Was that Latin? Good heavens, I haven't heard anything like it since I was at university. Where's he from?"

"England, but he only speaks Latin," Malcolm said, then added with a whisper, "He's a little eccentric."

"Curious," David said. Then, with a lot of stammering, David asked Arthur in Latin what he was doing in America.

Arthur unleashed his answer in a flood of words.

David held up his hands in surrender. "Whoa, wait. Slow down. What's he saying?"

Malcolm explained, "We're in a difficult situation. Arthur's a British subject, but he doesn't have any identification to prove it. We're trying to get him back to England."

David eyed Malcolm suspiciously. "Who are you working for these days, Malcolm?"

"Working for?" Malcolm asked.

David smiled. "You don't have to tell me. Forgive me for asking." He looked at Alan and Arthur with a new respect.

"Hold on, David. It's not what you think," Malcolm said, certain that David thought they were working for the government on a top-secret operation. "I'm not working for anyone. This is my problem. I just need a British passport for Arthur."

"Yeah, I saw the new directives," David said softly.

"New directives?"

"Red tape on all sides. Your agents can't issue our passports without our okay. I understand completely."

"I'm not sure you do," Malcolm said.

David winked. "Maybe I can speed things up. Come down to my office at the British Embassy."

David and Malcolm walked on ahead to the front door that led back to roar of traffic on Massachusetts Avenue.

Arthur asked Alan what they were doing.

"We needed a miracle," Alan said with a shrug. "It looks like God gave us the British Secret Service."

Sheriff Hounslow and two of his officers were waiting for Malcolm, Alan, and Arthur when they stepped from the plane onto the tarmac.

"Hello, Sheriff." Malcolm forced a smile. "What brings you here?"

Hounslow jabbed a finger at Arthur. "He does. We've been looking all over for him. Imagine my surprise to find out that he's with you."

Arthur's entire body stiffened as if he might lunge at the sheriff. Alan put a restraining hand on Arthur's arm.

"I don't understand. You're acting as though he's a fugitive," Alan said.

"In a way he is. The doctors at the hospital want him transported to Hancock because his violent behavior poses a threat to the public—"

"Oh, Sheriff, that's nonsense and you know it."

"I know no such thing," Hounslow snapped. "My car's going to be in the shop for a week from chasing this lunatic."

"Nobody asked you to chase him. He was on my property at the time, if I remember correctly."

"Exactly. So maybe I should take you in as an accessory."

"Accessory to what?"

"To . . . harboring a fugitive. Resisting arrest."

"That's ridiculous. Now, if you'll excuse us, we're going back to my house."

"You can go back to your house, but His Highness here is going back to the hospital. I'm not keen to have him wandering the streets of Fawlt Line."

"Sheriff, if you'll only leave him in my care, he won't be wandering anywhere except out of here. We've made plans for him to—"

"Don't bother explaining, Malcolm. He's going to the hospital first while we figure out who's going to pay for the damage to my car."

"Good grief. I'll pay for the damage to your car. Just let us go. After tomorrow he won't even be here."

"We'll see about that," Hounslow said and reached for Arthur. "Come along. We don't want a scene."

Arthur didn't move.

Hounslow groaned. "He's not going to be difficult, is he? Tell him in whatever gibberish he's speaking to come along quietly."

Malcolm began, "Richard—"

"Let's go, Your Eminence." Hounslow gave Arthur's arm a tug.

Arthur suddenly roared and threw his entire weight into Hounslow, knocking the wind out of him. The sheriff fell to the ground with a thud.

"Arthur! No!" Malcolm shouted.

The two officers jumped at Arthur, but he anticipated their move and quickly grabbed one of them by the shirt collar and swung him around with a bone-crunching thump into the other.

"Stop, Arthur, stop!" Alan yelled to Arthur in Latin.

At the sound of the Latin, Arthur turned. One of the officers leapt onto his back. Arthur toppled and fell to the tarmac. In an instant, the other officer was also on top of him. Hounslow joined in the fray.

"Stop!" Malcolm shouted again and again. "He doesn't understand!"

The three men managed to get Arthur turned over onto his stomach and wrenched his hands to a position where they could snap the handcuffs on his wrists.

"Sheriff, listen to me!"

Hounslow and his men dragged Arthur to the car, being careful not to let him get a proper footing, and dumped him into the back of the first police cruiser. He fought against them, but they managed to get the door closed. Arthur roared again from inside.

Hounslow checked the torn knee on his trousers, then looked

accusingly at Malcolm. "Look at what he did. This isn't helping his case, you know."

"He doesn't understand," Malcolm said. "He has no point of reference for what you're doing to him."

"Then I guess he'll learn really fast, won't he?" Hounslow said and got into his car. He slammed the door. Arthur sat up behind him and threw his head against the security screen. He shouted something unintelligible at Hounslow.

With Malcolm and Alan watching from the tarmac, Hounslow stepped on the gas and sped away with lights and siren going full force.

"Adam—" Malcolm began.

Judge Adam Marks wadded up a piece of paper and threw it at the trash can like a basketball. It hit the rim and bounced to the floor. "I've been robbed."

"Adam, please."

Adam sighed as he swiveled around in his chair. "He attacked the sheriff and his men, for heaven's sake. What do you want me to do?" He tugged at the folds of his robe and put his feet up on his desk.

"Get him out. Put him in my custody," Malcolm said.

The judge laughed. "Do the words 'fat chance' mean anything to you?"

"Why? The hospital can't help him—and neither can time in jail. He doesn't even belong here!"

"From everything I've heard, he's exactly where he belongs," Adam declared, wadding up another piece of paper. "The psychiatric ward at the hospital is ideal."

"He's not crazy."

"He thinks he's King Arthur, and he gives every indication of being a public nuisance—a violent public nuisance." Adam tossed the paper at the trash can. "Two points!"

"That's only because he doesn't realize what's going on. Drop yourself 1500 years into the past and see how *you* cope."

Adam smiled at Malcolm. "Aha—so you *do* think he's King Arthur. I should've known. Somebody's going to lock *you* up one of these days."

Malcolm changed his approach. "Adam, listen to me. Do you pretend to understand everything there is about this world?"

"No," Adam said.

"Then you admit that there are things beyond our comprehension."

"Yeah, sure," Adam said indifferently.

"Then use your imagination for a minute—the way you did when we were in school together. Remember those wild stories you used to make up about space travel and time travel?"

"That was high school—my grade in English depended on those wild stories," Adam said, tucking his hands behind his head. "This is reality."

"And we don't know everything there is to know about reality. That's my point!" Malcolm said.

Adam rolled his eyes heavenward. "Here comes the lecture."

"If necessary," Malcolm nodded. "You're a churchgoing man. You know that there's more to reality than what we see with our eyes, touch with our hands, experience from one second to the next. There's an *eternal* reality. A reality that slips outside the boundaries of time and space."

"But—"

"You believe that death is just a doorway to that eternal reality, right?"

"Right, but—"

"Okay, so what if there are other kinds of doors leading to other realities—realities of different places in time—past and present all mixed up in that big house called eternity?"

"Malcolm—"

"And what if the many doors in that house are usually locked. But one day, the house settles a little and one of the doors cracks open and whatever was in that room slips out into the hall—into our time."

"Those are a lot of 'what ifs', Malcolm."

"Life is full of 'what ifs', Adam."

"Look, if you're standing here expecting me to believe that Time suddenly belched and out came King Arthur, I can't do it."

Malcolm sighed. "All right, don't believe it. Just administer some justice and let me take Arthur to England."

Adam spread his hands is surrender. "I can't. He's too hot right now. What'll people say if I hand down a decision letting that man loose after he assaults our police officers? Jerry Anderson is already having a field day with this in the *Gazette*. Releasing him will only add fuel to the fire."

"What are you suggesting?" Malcolm asked.

"Leave it alone for now," Adam said, shrugging. "Let the doctors perform their tests and write up their evaluation. If he's sane, they'll say so. Then maybe, in a week or two, I'll release him to your custody. Deal?"

"A week or two! I'm not sure we have that long."

"Why wouldn't you?" Adam asked. "Is he on some kind of schedule?"

"I'm not certain. But he's . . . aging."

"Aging?"

"Yes." Malcolm tugged at his ear. "He's in the wrong place at the wrong time, and I think it's affecting him somehow."

Adam grinned. "And you think a trip abroad will help him."

"It'll have to. If going to England isn't why he's here, then we're all in big trouble." Malcolm tried not to sound melodramatic, but he spoke very seriously. "The past as we know it could change."

"How?"

Malcolm didn't dare try to answer.

Adam thought about it for a moment, then shook his head. "Sorry, Malcolm. I can't let him out. He'll have to hang on for at least a week."

Alan reached Malcolm's cottage as the sun made its final descent to the horizon. Weatherwise, it had been a perfect day, but Alan hadn't seen any of it. After the ambush at the airport, he spent the rest of the afternoon persuading the sheriff to allow him into the psych ward to see Arthur. "I'm the only one who can talk to him," Alan reasoned. Hounslow eventually agreed.

Alan didn't like what he saw. Arthur had been heavily medicated and restrained with straps. Lines were etched deeply around his eyes, his mouth was drawn, his hair was a wiry gray.

Alan pulled up a chair next to the bed. Arthur signaled for him to lean closer. He whispered drowsily in Latin that he needed Alan to do something for him.

"What is your pleasure, Your Majesty?" Alan asked.

Arthur told him, and Alan left the hospital immediately and went straight to Malcolm's cottage.

"Mr. Dubbs isn't here. I think he went to see the judge," Mrs. Packer said when she answered the door. "But your daughter is inside with Jeff. They're in the study."

Jeff and Elizabeth sat on the sofa laughing at some private joke. Alan observed them silently from the doorway for a moment. They had been best of friends before their adventure in an alternative time a few months before. But the trauma and near loss they experienced took them from the love shared by two friends to the love shared by soul mates. It was as if their hearts had gone through an intense white fire that had left them melted together in pure unity.

Their adventure in time had deepened Alan's love for them as well, particularly for Elizabeth. Alan thought he had lost his daughter then—and to have her come back had renewed his faith in her and in God. He had always given an academic assent to Time's place in a larger, eternal scheme. What happened to Elizabeth clinched it for him in a heartfelt way. And, not surprisingly, it was his belief in her experience that allowed him to believe in King Arthur's appearance now.

"Daddy?" Elizabeth had turned to face her father. "We were waiting for you. Is everything all right?"

"Hi," he said with artificial brightness. It didn't fool anybody. He slumped down into the chair next to them.

"What's wrong, Mr. Forde?" Jeff asked.

Alan washed a hand over his face. "I'm just a little tired."

"We heard what happened at the airport. How's King Arthur?" Elizabeth asked anxiously.

"Not very well, I'm afraid to say." Alan breathed deeply. "God help the poor man. It's bad enough being thrown into the future, but to be handcuffed, dragged around, and thrown into a psychiatric ward . . ." Alan shivered involuntarily.

"You look pale, Daddy. Maybe you should rest for a while," Elizabeth suggested.

"I can't. Arthur asked me to do something for him."

"What?"

"He wants his sword and clothes taken back to the church ruin," Alan explained wearily. "He said it's where they belong. They're not safe anywhere else. He's afraid of what might happen if Excalibur falls into the wrong hands."

Jeff was on his feet instantly. "I can do it."

"*We* can do it," Elizabeth corrected him.

Alan nodded his approval, relieved to have someone else share his burden. "Here's what you have to do. . . ."

They reverently placed Arthur's carefully cleaned and folded clothes (compliments of Mrs. Packer) in the back seat of Jeff's Volkswagen Bug. The sword had to be angled in to fit.

"Be careful," Alan said as they pulled away amidst the loud sputter and pop of Jeff's car.

"Why did he say that?" Jeff asked, wondering if there was a potential danger he wasn't aware of.

Elizabeth shrugged. "That was just Dad being Dad. He's been

like that ever since we got back." "We got back" was the phrase they used to refer to their time travel.

Things had changed at the church ruin since they were last there. Outside, a large truck was parked next to the barricade entrance, obviously left by the construction workers who'd been there throughout the day. Inside, new scaffolding had been built along two of the walls. Jeff lugged the sword like a pair of skis on his shoulder. Elizabeth carried the clothes and a large flashlight.

"I don't like this," she said in response to the dancing shadows and the eerie cryptlike appearance of the church.

"I just hope they didn't move the stone table," Jeff said.

Elizabeth dodged one of the pillars and moved the flashlight around like a spotlight. She pointed. "There it is." It was hiding on the other side of a stack of lumber.

They approached the stone table and stared at it silently for a moment. Jeff felt a strong urge to pray, but was afraid that Elizabeth might think he was being dramatic. He had no idea that Elizabeth was feeling the same thing.

"It looks like a coffin," she said and shivered.

"Quit scaring yourself."

"What did King Arthur want us to do?" she asked.

Jeff moved around to the side of the table. "According to your father, we need to move the top to one side. It's like a big, hollow stone box, I guess. We're supposed to hide his stuff inside."

"Then what?"

"That's all."

Elizabeth frowned. "But what if a worker finds it?"

Jeff shrugged. "It wasn't my idea."

"Maybe we should hide them somewhere else, somewhere safer. We could take them to my house," Elizabeth offered.

"He didn't say to take it to your house, Bits," Jeff said, invoking his pet name for her. "He said specifically to put it in here."

"But why?"

"Your dad didn't say. Maybe Arthur didn't say. Maybe he figures since this is where he came in, it's also the way out."

"But what if nobody figured that construction workers are crawling around here all day long?" Elizabeth implored him. "I'll bet your Uncle Malcolm wouldn't let us do this."

"Maybe he wouldn't," Jeff said, exasperated, "and maybe we'll ask him when we see him later. We can always come back for it. Meanwhile, we do what the king asked us to do, okay?"

"I don't like it."

"You'll get over it." Jeff leaned against the lid of the table and pushed. It didn't move. "It's heavy, that's for sure," he said and pushed again.

Elizabeth positioned the flashlight on the pallet, then wrapped her hands clawlike over the edge and pulled from the other side. The top jerked loose with a loud scrape, then slid at a painfully slow rate to one side.

"That's enough," Jeff gasped as he collapsed against the flat stone. He wiped away the beads of sweat on his brow with the back of his hand.

Elizabeth bent down and retrieved the bundle of clothes. She placed them inside the table, then suddenly shivered. "It gives me the creeps," she said.

"I know," Jeff nodded. With a grunt, he picked up Excalibur and slid it into the box next to the clothes. Again, they both fell silent. Jeff felt like they should say something. He looked across the table at Elizabeth.

Her eyes were fixed on the dark hole inside the box.

"Bits?" Jeff asked uneasily. He didn't like the vacant expression that had passed over her face.

She tilted her head to the left slightly.

"Bits," Jeff said. "I think we better get out of here." He pulled on the stone lid.

"*Vale: oremus semper,*" she said. It was almost a sigh.

Jeff looked at her, wide-eyed. "What did you say?"

Startled, Elizabeth put her hand to her mouth. "Huh?"

"What did you just say?"

She looked stricken. "I don't know. That was so weird."

"It sounded like King Arthur's language. You said something in Latin!"

"Did I?" Elizabeth asked nervously. She wrapped her arms around herself. "Hurry up, Jeff. I don't want to stay here. It's scaring me."

"Okay. Help me." He and Elizabeth pushed the lid back into place. Certain that it was secure, they headed for the doorway.

What made them turn around for a last look at the table before they left, they didn't know. It might have been the strange hum that seemed to work its way into their consciousness. Perhaps it was the fog that suddenly swirled at their feet like dry ice at a rock concert. Or it could have been the peculiar green light reflected on the walls in front of them. Likely, it was all of the above. They stopped dead in their tracks and looked behind them.

The stone table was ablaze with green and yellow light that came from *inside* the table. It glowed through the sides and top, as if the box were made of glass instead of stone. Jeff blinked and Elizabeth rubbed her eyes to be sure they were actually seeing the clothes and the sword through the thick rock.

As if someone had turned up the juice, the light grew brighter and brighter until it was a blinding brilliant white.

"Turn away!" Jeff called out as he put his hands up to protect himself.

Elizabeth covered her face and caught the scream that rose in her throat.

Then it stopped. The light went out, the hum faded, and even the fog raced in patches like white mice to the corners of the church.

Jeff grabbed the flashlight from Elizabeth and rushed to the stone table.

"Don't, Jeff, please!" she cried out.

With all the adrenaline now surging through his body, he pushed on the lid with all his might. It moved more easily this time. He shined the beam of the flashlight into the dark box.

"Jeff, what was that? What happened?"

Jeff looked up at Elizabeth. "It's empty. The things are gone."

CHAPTER 16

"Well, now, look at you." Ponsonby smiled graciously as he walked into the garage, where Adrian was polishing the Rolls Royce.

He'd been working for Ponsonby almost a week. His job initially, as his immediate boss Lewis explained the first day, was to polish the exteriors of the cars and treat the leather interiors. Simple mechanical work—changing the oil and brake fluids and the like—was also his to do. But the pay was surprisingly generous and Adrian figured that, if nothing else, he could work a few weeks and use the money to take a nice long trip for the rest of the summer.

"Lewis tells me you're doing excellent work," Ponsonby said. He walked back and forth along the fronts of the cars like a general inspecting his troops. "From the looks of things, I agree."

"Thank you, Mr. Ponsonby," Adrian said proudly.

Ponsonby had shown a keen interest in Adrian all week, stopping by frequently to chat. All subjects were fair game. He asked Adrian about his childhood, his interests, his hopes and dreams. Interspersed with the questions were Ponsonby's observations about life.

For example, "If you let it, all the baggage of your childhood can cripple you for life. A slight on the schoolyard, a bully who wouldn't leave you alone, hurt feelings, lost love . . . they can come back to haunt you as an adult and impair your ability to make sensible decisions. Suddenly you're cowering in front of your competitors the way you did in front of that bully. But once you realize you have the baggage, you can get rid of it. You can overcome the past to conquer your future."

Adrian was getting a crash course in Ponsonby Maxims, but he didn't mind. Ponsonby made good sense. His ideas and comments gripped feelings in Adrian he didn't even know he had. He made Adrian feel as though things were possible. Fortunes could be attained, dreams could be made realities. One just had to have the inner resources. The old cliché seemed true: *I'm the master of my fate*, Adrian thought.

Unfortunately, Adrian couldn't help but make comparisons between Ponsonby and his own father. Where Ponsonby was charismatic and aggressive, Graham Peters was gentle and sensitive. Where Ponsonby made hard decisions—that usually turned out to be right—Graham waffled on most decisions, thinking them through to the last degree, and even then they didn't amount to much. The truth was: Adrian loved his father but . . . wouldn't he rather be like Ponsonby?

"Montague, my valet, has a mother who's gone in hospital in York," Ponsonby said. "I'd like you to fill in for him while he's away. It may only be a week or so."

Adrian dropped the polishing cloth. "Me? I've never been a valet before. I don't know the first thing about it."

"Are you telling me you can't learn, or are you saying that you don't want to do it?" Ponsonby asked with that challenging look in his eyes.

"Of course, I want to do it, but—"

"If you want to, then you'll learn quickly. If I were worried about your ability, I wouldn't have asked. I'm asking because I have every confidence in you. A valet is nothing more than a personal assistant," Ponsonby asserted. "There'll be extra pay, of course. Will you do it?"

"Yes, sir."

"Good. Lewis will go home with you to get your things."

Adrian was confused. "Get my things?"

"Yes," Ponsonby said. "If you're going to be my valet, you'll have to move in."

"So, you see, your Arthur character is crazy as a loon. He attacked some policemen, and they put him in a mental ward," Graham said, referring to the small article he'd found in the back of the morning paper.

Myrddin fingered the clipping. "Not necessarily. Just because they locked him up doesn't mean they're right."

Graham smiled. "Well, if Arthur's come back to make a good impression, he's started off on the wrong foot."

"I don't believe Arthur has come back to make a good impression," Myrddin said seriously.

"Then why did he—I mean, hypothetically speaking, if such a thing were remotely possible—why *would* he come back?"

"He would come back to help make things right."

"Cure social ills? Start a charity?" Graham inquired. His tone was glib.

"Perhaps."

Graham pressed on. "What do you think, that he'll come back to be our king again? Don't you think our current monarch might be a bit cheesed off at the intrusion? I can see the two of them now, battling over who'll attend the opening of the new shopping center or christen the ship."

Myrddin pointed a warning finger at him. "Don't be disrespectful."

"Then what do you think Arthur will do?" Graham asked. "Lead England to newfound victory somewhere? Restore the glory of Camelot? Wave Excalibur a few times and bring back the Empire?"

Myrddin shook his head. "You're thinking in very obvious terms, Graham. What is England's greatest need?"

Graham shrugged. "Most would say it's the economy. Will he come back to become the Chancellor of the Exchequer?"

"No," Myrddin sighed. "I thought that you, of all people, would know the answer."

Graham frowned, feeling as if he'd failed a test he hadn't even known he was taking. "Sorry. I don't think there is an answer because Arthur isn't coming back. It's a fantasy, Myrddin. A myth."

"Not all myths are untrue, Graham," Myrddin declared.

"Maybe not," he responded harshly. "But I don't have time for myths, true or untrue. I have reality to deal with. I have a collapsing church, a struggling parish, and a wayward son. Indulge in the legends of King Arthur if you want to, but don't expect me to stop my life to play along."

Myrddin didn't say anything.

Suddenly Graham blushed. "I'm sorry, Myrddin. I don't know where that came from."

"It came from your heart," Myrddin said softly.

"Yes, it did. That's what scares me."

"Go home, Graham," Myrddin said with a wave of his hand, but not in an unkind tone. "Go home to your realities."

Adrian had put a suitcase into the back of Lewis's car when Graham pulled into the driveway. With a glance at his father, Adrian went back into the house.

Graham got out of his car and walked to the driver's side of the beige Land Rover. "Hello, Lewis," Graham said to the leprechaun-like face just inside the window, cigarette dangling from its lips.

" 'lo, Reverend," Lewis nodded.

"So . . . what's all this then?"

"Adrian's moving in with Ponsonby," Anne spoke up from the kitchen doorway. "I've already talked to him. There's nothing we can do."

"What do you mean there's nothing we can do. We're his parents. Adrian!" he called out.

"Hello, Dad," Adrian said casually as he slipped past his mother and brought an armload of books to the car.

"Your mother tells me you're moving out—and in with Ponsonby."

"Not permanently. He just needs me for a couple of weeks," Adrian replied and tossed the books in the back. He closed the door.

"You could have asked first."

"Why? Would you have said yes?"

"We might have, after some consideration," Graham answered.

"I didn't have a month for your considerations," Adrian said. "Ponsonby needed to know right away."

"He doesn't have a phone?"

"Is there something wrong, Dad? It's a straightforward job. It pays well. You won't miss me. You can pretend I'm away at school again."

"That's not what I'm talking about," Graham said and took Adrian by the arm to lead him away from the car and Lewis. "You know how uneasy I felt about your working for Ponsonby at all. He's an unscrupulous man. He spins little webs, and you could easily get caught in one. He'll pull you in, Adrian. Let's be honest about this. He stands for everything we're against—or should I say that he's against everything we stand for."

"And what's that, Dad? What do you stand for? The old church? The archdeacon?"

"Adrian!" Anne snapped from the doorway.

"I'm just asking, since we're being honest. You talk about standing for something, and I don't know what it is. I don't see it. At least you know with Mr. Ponsonby. He doesn't sit around wringing his hands about things that don't matter. He's *doing* something with his life. Maybe he'll help me do something with mine. Which is a lot more than some people have done."

Graham was speechless.

Anne strode toward Adrian from the doorway, crossing the gap in only a few long steps. "That's a terrible thing to say! You apologize to your father!"

Adrian looked away.

"I mean it!" Anne said.

"It's all right, darling," Graham said quietly. "He was speaking his heart. Go to Ponsonby if that's what you want." Graham walked into the house.

Anne was aghast. "You can go," she said angrily. "But I'm not sure you should come back until you learn to respect your father. He's a good man, and what you just said was. . . was . . ." Her words were choked off by angry tears. She spun around and marched into the house, slamming the door behind her.

Adrian grimaced and climbed into the car.

CHAPTER 17

"A perfect cup of tea. Thank you, Mrs. Packer," David Jenkins said happily.

Mrs. Packer nodded. "You're welcome," she said and whisked out of the room.

Malcolm sipped his tea. "I appreciate your driving all this way, David. You didn't have to do it. I could've flown down again."

"I needed time away from the city anyway," David said with a smile. "It's lovely country you have in this part of the state. Besides, I wanted to deliver this personally." He handed over a small brown envelope. "It's for your 'friend.' "

Malcolm took the envelope and opened it up. Inside was a passport. It had a photo of Arthur—taken the day they were at the British Embassy—and the name Arthur Pendragon, complete with appropriate biographical and administrative details to give him safe passage into England. "David," Malcolm said appreciatively.

"You know that you must only use it this one time, then destroy it," David cautioned him.

"Uh-huh," Malcolm answered. He wasn't a novice when it came to this sort of work. He flipped through the pages. Some bore the immigration stamps of England, France, the United States, and Hong Kong.

"Those stamps give him a well-traveled appearance. Less chance of being questioned. My boss insisted on it."

"Your boss?" Malcolm asked warily. "You told someone else about this?"

"Of course. I can't just create passports without clearance. He was happy to do it once I told him about your work with my father."

Malcolm winced. "David, you're making me feel very guilty."

"Nonsense. Your man needs to get to England, and I'm happy to help."

"I know, but you think you're helping me with an Intelligence matter. You think 'my man' is an agent," Malcolm said.

"You don't have to explain," David said pleasantly and took another drink of his tea.

"But I do. We're not on the kind of mission you think. This has nothing to do with Intelligence. I tried to tell you at the embassy, but . . ." Malcolm was at a loss for words. "I'm sorry."

David looked uncomfortable. "Then what's this all about?"

Malcolm took a deep breath and decided, for better or worse, to tell him everything. "Mrs. Packer," he called out. "I think you'd better bring a fresh pot of tea."

Alan was worried. Arthur looked at least twenty years older than he had when he first arrived in Fawlt Line. His strength and vibrancy had dimmed to a near feeble state. He barely spoke and, when he did, it was in a hoarse whisper. The doctors didn't bother to restrain his arms anymore. He lay in his hospital bed like any other mentally ill geriatric patient.

Alan wished Malcolm were allowed in to see him, to impress upon him the urgency of the situation. But Sheriff Hounslow had left strict instructions that Alan Forde was the only one permitted to see the patient.

"Can't you release him now?" Alan asked Dr. Carey, the supervisor of the psychiatric ward.

"No," Dr. Carey replied. His lean face reminded Alan of a greyhound's. "Our tests aren't complete. We're dealing with an extremely advanced form of dementia."

"But can't you see what being here is doing to him?"

"This is a hospital, Mr. Forde. If he's ill, this is the best place for him to be."

Alan bit back the sharp retort he wanted to make and returned to Arthur's room. Malcolm knew the score, Alan reasoned. If there were any way to get Arthur out of this hospital, he'd try it.

"How do you feel, Your Majesty?" Alan asked in Latin.

"I am plagued by dreams," Arthur answered. "I see my kingdom crumbling beneath the treachery of Mordred."

Alan remembered how Arthur and Mordred killed each other in that last decisive battle, and Camelot went the way of all dreams. He bit his lip. What would happen to history if Arthur died here and now in present-day Fawlt Line?

He changed the subject. "Much has been written about the Holy Grail, my lord. Would you be gracious enough to tell me what really happened?"

At the mention of the Grail, Arthur's face lit up. "The Grail belonged to Joseph of Arimathea, my ancestor, who brought my country to the knowledge of the salvation of our Lord Jesus Christ. It was the dish used by our Lord Himself at the final feast with His disciples, before His betrayal, crucifixion and, thanks be to God, His resurrection. Alas, I never saw it. I cannot tell you where it came from or where it went, though we knew it to be hidden within our shores."

"Why did you send your knights to find it?"

"As Merlin had prophesied years before, my kingdom became plagued by great evil, my barons fighting against each other for land, knights fighting knights for mere sport; murder and thievery abounding. Some even forsook Christ Himself and turned to an evil faith and cruel worship of the pagan gods of Britain. These evils threatened to tear the kingdom to pieces. So I beseeched my kinsman, the archbishop, "Tell me how to rid my country of evil." He said that the Grail must be found, for with it would come healing for my land."

He paused to catch his breath, then continued. "I assembled my knights at the Round Table, of which you have heard, and spoke to them of our country's great need. Sir Gawaine, a most valiant knight, rose up and vowed his very life to find the Grail. Then the rest of my knights, moved by Gawaine's passion, made avowal also. The next day they rode from Camelot with great fanfare. Yet I was heavy of heart, for I knew that many would never return.

"For two years my knights searched the land for the Grail, battling evil where they found it. As I feared, many died, while others grew sick at heart and gave up the quest. It came about that three courageous knights encountered one another in their travels and determined to ride together to find the Grail. They were Sir Galahad, Sir Perceval, and Sir Bors. They performed many marvelous deeds, and in time united many of the barons of the Northern Lands against the pagans.

"One morning, they came upon a castle on a great cliff of Scotland. It was besieged by evil and cruel pagan knights. Earl Hernox, the lord of the castle, was taken prisoner. His daughter Issyllt escaped and beseeched the three good knights to rescue her father. Being good and virtuous men, they agreed. No sooner had they given consent, than the evil knights swarmed upon them from the castle itself. It was folly for the evil knights. So great were the valor and fierceness of Galahad, Perceval, and Bors that their blows could not be withstood. The evil knights were driven back into the castle, and my three knights pursued them until all were slain."

Again Arthur paused. Alan asked him if he wanted to stop. Arthur shook his head and continued. "The three looked upon the many dead and grew sober, thinking themselves great sinners for their deeds. Earl Hernox, filled with cheer and joy at the reunion with his daughter and the restoration of his castle, tried to comfort them that theirs was a just cause. Suddenly, they beheld before them a priest, dressed in white and great with age. Galahad, Perceval, and Bors knelt before him, and he assured them of absolution once the dead were buried and the halls cleansed of all violence. My knights vowed to do so.

"When all had been done as the priest commanded, Earl Hernox and his daughter were asked to leave the three knights alone in the room. Suddenly the doors slammed shut, all went dark, and a loud, rushing wind arose as if making a mournful cry. Though terrified, my knights did not flee. Then a bright light filled the room, so dazzling that it was painful to look at, yet my knights could not help themselves. For through the light they saw a beautifully laid table, and upon the table was a wide dish of silver.

"Then the doors opened, and men with the countenance of angels appeared. They moved to and from the table as if laying it for a great banquet. When it seemed as though their task was completed, a marvelously old man, dressed as a bishop, appeared at the side of the table. On the breast of his robe were written the words 'Joseph, Who Did Take Our Lord's Body from the Cross.'

"The knights were troubled by this apparition of Joseph of Arimathea, the first bishop of Christendom in Britain and a man dead for more than five hundred years! Seeing their consternation, the bishop smiled upon them and said, 'Marvel not, good knights, for though I am but a spirit, I have come to help you.'

"The bishop bade them eat from the silver dish upon the table, and it was the sweetest, most marvelous food they had ever eaten. After this, the bishop asked them if they knew what the vessel was from which they had eaten. The knights said they knew not. The bishop told them that it was the holy vessel out of which our Lord ate before He was betrayed and killed on the cross. He redeemed the world if men would but choose His way.

"Sir Galahad exclaimed that it was the Holy Grail, the very thing they most desired to see. The bishop, who had spoken to them in a sweet and pleasant manner, then spoke with sorrow in his voice. 'So you shall see it. But none other of your kind will ever see it. On this night it will depart from your land.' The three knights wept grievously, for without the Grail, they knew their king and country were lost. Good Sir Galahad asked if there was nothing they could do to keep the Grail and turn the land from its wicked ways. The bishop said sadly that there was not. 'Have you not tried for two years to rid the land of its evil? Were not your labors and battling in vain? No, it is the will of God that this land and its people be abandoned to their own evil devices. Sorrow, death, treachery, and rebellion will come at the hands of those who live to seek only fortune and profit. The pagans will try to blot out the very memory of God and Christ. The sanctuaries of prayers will become lairs of wolves. Owls will nest where hymns of praise were sung. Doom and desolation will fill the hearts of all, for there will be no godly comfort to aid them.' "

"You have just described our modern world," Alan said sadly.

Arthur went on with his story. "The bishop turned to Galahad and Perceval and said that inasmuch as they were pure and unspotted from evil, their souls would go with him when he departed. He then looked upon Sir Bors and said that he would live to fight for Christ yet awhile longer and to tell the king all he had seen and heard. Suddenly a blinding light filled the room, and Sir Bors fell backward from the table. After a time the light faded, and Sir Bors saw Galahad and Perceval on their knees where the table had been. But, going to the two knights, he discerned that the spirit had departed from them. They fell over dead.

"Sir Bors, with a sorrowful heart, entreated Earl Hernox to bury the good knights. Then Bors returned to Camelot and told me all that had happened. I and my remaining knights wept openly for the loss of the age and the terror that would one day come. I still fight for the good, Alan, and for the glory of Camelot, but evil presses in and I am weary."

A tear slid down Arthur's cheek. "God grant that this dream would end now, for I am heavy of heart."

"Your Majesty," Alan began sympathetically, but was interrupted by a commotion outside of the room. He stood up just as the door was flung open by a pale-faced Officer Massey, who had been assigned to keep guard at Arthur's door. A young man in a dark suit and jet black sunglasses strode into the room.

"What's going on?" Alan asked.

"This is the man," the young man announced in a clipped British accent.

Dr. Carey, who followed hot on his heels, stammered, "But you can't just take him."

The young man, who was David Jenkins, turned on him. "Is it normally your policy to argue with the British Secret Service? Must I show you my badge again?"

"No, of course not," Carey blubbered, "but don't you need some kind of warrant or subpoena or official paperwork?"

David leaned toward him, his jaw set so tight that Alan could see the muscles working. "Oh, you'll get paperwork, all right. The lot of you may be indicted for harboring this fugitive. Can he walk?"

"Yes," Carey said. "We think so."

David pointed to Alan. "I understand you're his translator. Help me take him out."

Confused, Alan whispered to Arthur that they were leaving, and helped him to his feet.

"Maybe I should call the sheriff," Officer Massey offered.

"And put it out all over your radio waves that I'm here? Are you mad?" David cried out. "Are you trying to cause an international incident?"

"No, sir." Officer Massey retreated.

"Get his clothes," David said to Alan. Alan nodded, rushed to the wardrobe and grabbed what he could. "We'll have him change in the car. Time is of the essence."

"I'd still like to make a call," Dr. Carey said nervously.

"If you're willing to risk a national emergency, fine, call whomever you like—*five minutes after we leave*," David barked.

Carey agreed.

With Arthur between them, David and Alan went down the hall, through the security door, and to the rear stairwell. David's car was parked at the back door. They helped Arthur into the back seat. Alan got in the passenger side, and David pointed a threatening finger at Dr. Carey, who was fluttering nearby. "I wasn't here. You never saw me. Providing you love your country."

Dr. Carey nodded his head vigorously.

David got into the car, started it up, and pulled away with a dramatic screech of his tires against the pavement.

"What in the world is going on?" Alan asked, once they'd cleared the hospital grounds and were well on their way out of Fawlt Line.

David exhaled, and his whole tough-guy demeanor evaporated. "I'm going to lose my job, *that's* what's going on."

"But . . . where are you taking us?"

"To the airport. You have a plane to catch."

"The *British* Secret Service?" Hounslow bellowed. The veins in his neck stood out. A throbbing pulse was visible on his forehead. "Did you get the agent's name?"

"Not really. He flashed his badge and . . . it happened so fast," Officer Massey replied.

"I'm sure it did."

"I didn't know what else to do," Officer Massey said.

Hounslow rubbed his face and ran his fingers through his thinning hair. "Malcolm's behind this. I just know it."

"They probably went to the airport. They'll take Malcolm's plane. Should we go after them?" Massey asked, wanting to come up with something to please his boss.

Hounslow sighed. "No. They're long gone by now."

"We could call the—"

"Let them go," Hounslow interrupted. "Good riddance to that maniac."

"Whatever you say." Massey slunk out of the office.

Hounslow hit his fist against the top of his desk. It wasn't losing Arthur. It wasn't even the ridiculous British Secret Service scam. More than anything, he hated for Malcolm Dubbs to get one up on him again.

Malcolm thanked David at the small Fawlt Line airport before they went their separate ways—David to his car; Malcolm with Alan, Jeff, and Arthur to Dulles Airport where they would catch the next commercial flight to London.

"Thank you, David. You have no idea what—"

"I don't want to know," David said with a hint of a smile. "From now on, this never happened. If anyone ever says I was involved, I'll deny it."

"Right."

"You'll burn his passport when you get to England."

"Understood."

"And you promise to go see my father while you're there."

"Absolutely."

David grabbed Malcolm's hand and shook it. "Call me when you get back. Maybe we can go out for a normal dinner, all right? Provided we're not in jail." He turned and walked across the tarmac to his car.

Malcolm climbed aboard his plane and taxied out for his take-off. "Everybody ready?"

A chorus of assent came back to him from the cabin.

"Then it's off to that green and pleasant land," Malcolm said and revved the engines.

This time Arthur didn't panic.

Alan didn't realize until they arrived at Dulles that his passport had expired three weeks before. Malcolm felt terrible that poor Alan, after working so hard, wouldn't get to see the end of the story—whatever that end might be. Alan merely smiled calmly and then explained to Arthur that he wouldn't be going with them.

Arthur was indignant. His face reflected his desire to throw a royal fit, to demand that Alan be allowed on the plane. But he was still weakened and didn't try. He suddenly embraced Alan. "If I had Excalibur, I would knight you. You are as courageous and true as the best of my knights. God grant I may return and do this very good thing for you," he said in Latin.

"Thank you, Your Majesty. God be with you."

Alan stood alone as Malcolm, Jeff, and Arthur walked through the security check for international flights. Arthur looked back one last time, a large but stooped old man, then smiled and waved sadly and disappeared around the corner.

CHAPTER 18

At 6:30 in the morning, the Boeing Triple-7 bumped gently as it landed on the airstrip at London's Heathrow airport. Arthur watched sleepily from his window seat as they taxied through an early morning fog toward the terminal. He breathed in deeply, as if he might take in some English air, then put his head back and closed his eyes again.

From the seat across the aisle, Malcolm wondered what was going through Arthur's mind. Without Alan, there was no way to communicate directly with him apart from obvious hand gestures. For the hundredth time Malcolm mentally kicked himself for not studying Latin in college. The cabin crew, clearly surmising that Arthur was senile, were sympathetic to the gray-haired old man who didn't speak English and didn't eat with utensils.

"We're here." Jeff smiled from his seat next to Arthur. "Any chance of getting a shower before we go anywhere?"

Malcolm nodded. "I'll get the rental car. We'll go straight to the hotel and get ourselves situated."

The plane pulled up to the gate, and Malcolm felt the butterflies stir to life in his stomach. Because Malcolm and Jeff had U. S. passports, they'd have to go through a line separate from Arthur. What if the Immigration Passport Control clerk decided to challenge Arthur? How would they communicate? Maybe they'd allow Malcolm to escort him through the British passport-holders' line. He could only hope . . . and pray.

Along with the rest of the passengers, the three of them walked the endless halls and moving walkways to Passport Control. It was an enormous room filled with travelers from all over the world, herded into several lines to accommodate their many different needs. A woman in an airport uniform stood at the entry point and directed questioners to the various lines. Malcolm approached her casually.

Malcolm said, "He's a British subject and —"

"That first line," she said, pointing.

"But we're not. We're Americans," Malcolm continued.

"You go in the second line," she said.

"But he doesn't speak English very well. Can we go with him through his line?"

"U. S. passports, you must go in the second line; British passport, he goes in the first," she said.

"But—"

She cut him off. "May I help the next person please?"

Malcolm put the British passport in Arthur's hands and gestured for him to go to the first line. Arthur clutched the passport with both hands as if he were afraid of dropping and breaking it. He strode off.

Malcolm and Jeff joined the line for foreign travelers, but Malcolm kept his eye on Arthur as they inched their way forward. The line for British citizens was much shorter.

"There he goes," Jeff gulped.

Arthur stepped forward to the desk. The clerk took his passport and said something. When Arthur merely smiled at him, the clerk shrugged, double-checked the photo with the face, flipped through some pages in a large binder, and waved him through. Arthur took the passport back and, spying Malcolm and Jeff again, walked around to wait for them on the other side of the restricted area. Malcolm and Jeff looked at each other and sighed.

Their relief was premature. A man in a suit walked up to Arthur and began speaking to him.

"What's this?" Malcolm exclaimed loud enough for a couple of people around him to turn and look.

Arthur, looking confused, took a few steps away from the man. The man followed and said something else to Arthur. Arthur looked at Malcolm helplessly, then turned on the man, shouted something at him in Latin and walked away. The man backed off for a moment, then persistently followed Arthur.

"Fifth podium, please," a man in an airport uniform said to Malcolm. He flicked a finger at Jeff, "Tenth podium, please."

Befuddled, Malcolm went to the immigration desk and impatiently answered the clerk's questions about why they were in Britain, how long they would be staying, and with whom they would be staying. Jeff did the same at the tenth podium. Both converged on Arthur and the stranger at the same time.

"It'll only take a minute," the man was saying when Malcolm and Jeff arrived.

"Excuse me. May I help you with something?" Malcolm asked with a strained friendliness.

"Who are you?" the man asked. "Are you with him?"

"Maybe you should tell us who *you* are first," Jeff said.

"Of course." The man fished around in his jacket pocket and produced a small billfold. He flipped it open to reveal credentials for a newspaper called *The London Post*. His name was Andy Samuelson. "Fair enough?"

"What do you want?" Malcolm asked, even less friendly now that he knew he was talking to a newspaperman and not an immigration official.

"I've been waiting for Michael Crockford. Do you know Michael Crockford?" the reporter asked.

"Should I?"

"He's a popular singer in Britain. Just appeared at a celebrity extravaganza for your president. You don't know him?"

"No."

Samuelson pushed a lock of his straight black hair away from his eyes. "Well, never mind. I'm meeting him for an exclusive interview—to pin down rumors about him and the president's daughter. Anyway, he was supposed to be on your plane, but he didn't show up. Or so I learned after waiting here for an hour."

"What's your point, Mr. Samuelson?" Malcolm asked.

"Well, I was sitting over there waiting, and I overheard the clerk say your friend's name: Arthur Pendragon. So I thought, Arthur *Pendragon*—as in *King* Arthur?—crumbs, I have to find out about this one. So I asked him to tell me about himself. Was he putting me on, or was that Latin he was shouting at me?"

"It was," Malcolm said. "But we're not interested in doing any interviews."

"What are you, his agent?"

"We're just friends who've had a very long flight. Now, if you'll excuse us—" Malcolm signaled for Arthur and Jeff to follow him as he brushed past the reporter.

Samuelson followed them. "Just tell me one thing: is that his real name or made up? Is he supposed to be a descendant of Arthur? Let's face it, there aren't a lot of Pendragons around."

"You asked *two* things. And we really don't have time," Malcolm said over his shoulder. They jumped on the escalator to go down to the baggage claim.

"Why won't you talk to me? It'd be a wonderful human interest story. He even *looks* like what I imagine Arthur would look like. Perhaps a bit older," Samuelson said from a few stairs up on the escalator.

Malcolm turned to him. "Would the immigration officials be pleased to know that you're badgering incoming passengers in a restricted area?"

"Now, now, don't get your knickers in a twist," Samuelson said.

"Then please leave us alone."

"Suit yourself," Samuelson said indifferently and strolled away from them at the bottom of the escalator.

"Persistent, wasn't he?" Jeff observed.

Malcolm agreed.

Jeff looked thoughtful as they walked to the baggage carousel. "Uncle Malcolm . . . why not talk to him? Maybe it would help with Arthur's mission. I mean, shouldn't King Arthur meet with the queen or the prime minister or somebody in charge?"

"Oh, you've figured out what his mission is?" Malcolm asked, a challenge in his voice. "You know that's what he should do?"

"No, but —"

"Jeff, until we have some clear leading, I don't want anyone to know who he is. I can't imagine anything more distracting than a media circus around him."

"Okay, okay," Jeff said defensively. "So what do we do now?"

"You get our luggage and go through customs while I get the rental car," Malcolm said. "Oh—and get some British money from the *bureau de change*. There are kiosks in the main terminal."

"Uh-huh. Then what?"

"The hotel—and the hope that something will happen to help us know what we're supposed to do next."

"You mean, like a phone call or a message left in our room?" Jeff smiled.

"Don't be a smart aleck," Malcolm said and walked off toward the exit through customs.

Jeff looked over at Arthur, who stood erect, his arms folded across his chest, his eyes fixed on the baggage coming down the ramp to the moving carousel. The sight of him looking as he did just then nearly made Jeff call Uncle Malcolm back. He needed a second opinion. Maybe it was Jeff's imagination, but Arthur seemed to be getting younger.

Jeff and Arthur cleared customs without incident, exchanged their dollars to pounds, and made their way to the curb in front of the terminal. Nothing in the roar of the traffic or the concrete parking garage straight ahead gave Jeff the impression that England was much different from America. He looked over at Arthur, who looked back and forth with an expression of incredulity. Just then a large double-decker bus drove past, belching black fumes. Arthur coughed violently and said something in Latin that sounded abusive. If Jeff could have understood, he'd have heard Arthur say that Lancelot's dragon smelled better than that monster.

"We have to wait for Uncle Malcolm," Jeff tried to say through words and gestures. He felt like a fool. Why couldn't Arthur speak English like the rest of his countrymen?

Arthur didn't look as though he wanted to wait for anyone. He paced restlessly back and forth, his hands in the pockets of the trousers Mrs. Packer had bought him.

He could be any business traveler, Jeff thought. Even the

disheveled hair and beard gave him an "eccentric wealthy" look. And there was no mistaking it in the sunlight: Jeff was certain that Arthur looked better, healthier.

Suddenly Arthur spoke with a tone of indignation and moved to the curb. Jeff smiled the smile people use when they don't know what to say to someone who speaks a foreign language, and gently pulled him back.

Twenty feet away, the automatic doors of the terminal whisked open, and the reporter, Andy Samuelson, stepped out onto the pavement. He frowned at the daylight and the time he'd wasted waiting for a celebrity who hadn't bothered to make his scheduled flight. Popping a piece of breath-freshening gum into his mouth, he glanced around and saw Jeff.

At that same moment, Jeff noticed the reporter. *Oh no*, he thought. He tried to think of a way to escape.

Just then, Samuelson called, "Is he supposed to do that?"

Jeff frowned at the reporter, who was now pointing at something behind Jeff. A horn blared. Jeff turned around in time to see Arthur crossing the road with complete disregard of the traffic.

"Your Highness!" Jeff cried out and raced after him.

With a screech, a car skidded to a halt in front of Jeff and nearly knocked him over. Jeff apologized quickly at the swearing driver and moved on toward Arthur, who was headed for a large green double-decker bus sitting at the curb. "Heathrow/Bristol Express" it said in large red letters on the side. Jeff was horrified to see Arthur step onto it.

"No!" Jeff shouted and stumbled for the bus. He plowed through the crowd of people waiting for other buses and shuttles and narrowly missed colliding with a woman pushing a baby in a stroller. "Wait!" he yelled.

The driver was just about to pull the bus door closed when Jeff leapt on.

"Is the big bloke with you?" the driver asked.

"Yeah," Jeff answered breathlessly, searching the rows of seats with his eyes.

"That'll be thirty quid," the driver said.

"What?"

The driver snorted impatiently. "Thirty *pounds*."

Confused, Jeff said, "But I don't belong on this bus."

"Obviously your friend thinks you do. C'mon, mate, we're on a tight schedule," he said. "Thirty pounds."

Jeff reached into his pocket and pulled out some money. He carefully picked away at the strange bills until he added up thirty and handed it over. Seeing Arthur toward the back of the bus, he headed down the aisle. Arthur was smiling contentedly.

"What are you doing?" Jeff asked. "We shouldn't be on this bus." He nearly lost his footing as the bus pulled away from the curb.

"Hold it," Jeff said. He turned to the tell the driver to stop, but Arthur suddenly grabbed his arm and pulled him into the seat. "What the—?"

He shook a finger at Jeff as if to say, "No."

"I've never been in England before. We don't know where we're going. What about Uncle Malcolm?" he asked.

Arthur smiled and patted Jeff's arm.

Jeff sank into the seat. *Uncle Malcolm isn't going to be happy about this.*

Malcolm pulled his rental car—a white Vauxhall—to the curb and searched the pockets of people for Jeff and Arthur. He didn't see them. As he climbed out of the car, he spied their suitcases sitting alone near the terminal wall. He rushed toward them, slowing when he saw Andy Samuelson standing nearby.

"I've been keeping the police from confiscating your bags," the reporter said. "They tend to assume that unaccompanied luggage contains bombs."

"Where are Jeff and Arthur?" Malcolm asked.

Samuelson grinned. "I hope you have a sense of humor."

Adrian knocked on Ponsonby's study door, then slipped inside. "You wanted to see me, sir?"

Ponsonby was standing at his desk with another man Adrian didn't know. "Ah, Adrian, just the man we need. Come in." The desk was covered with large sheets of paper. As Adrian got closer, he saw that they were maps; topographical maps, survey maps, and maps with notations written all over them.

Adrian felt a twinge of nervousness in his stomach.

"Do you know Mr. Clydesdale?" Ponsonby asked, and continued without waiting for an answer. "He is our liaison, if you will, with the various town councils. We've been considering new sites for my Superstores. Come look at these maps of the area."

Rounding the desk, Adrian looked down at the maps and wondered why he felt as though he were about to take an exam.

"Now, here are our choices. See if you can select the best site for one of our Superstores," Ponsonby said.

Adrian was right. It was a test. And, to his surprise, he cared deeply about not wanting to fail it.

Ponsonby rifled through the maps, then pointed to an area on one. "The farmers are actually quite keen to give up this one. But it's a run-off area that gets awfully soggy when it rains."

Adrian nodded in acknowledgment. He wanted to say something profound, but didn't want to sound like a poser. "I think you'd have drainage problems."

Ponsonby smiled as he gestured to another map. "This area is certainly agreeable, but it's remote."

"You'll have to spend a small fortune just to get a road to it, I suppose," Adrian offered.

"Exactly," Ponsonby smiled, then turned to another map. "This one is perfect, but we've been warned that some kind of rare hedgehog or whatever lives there."

Adrian rubbed his chin. This wasn't as hard as he thought.

"You'll battle environmental and animal rights groups every step of the way."

Ponsonby shot a knowing look at Mr. Clydesdale. "Didn't I tell you he was marvelous? Didn't I say what an instinct he has?" Ponsonby tossed a couple of maps aside, then rested his hand on another. It was a surveyor's map with numbers and codes scribbled all over it, but no identifying markings that Adrian recognized. "This one is the most promising. It's an area with two intersecting major roads, an ideal topography, and several major towns and cities within a twenty-mile radius. There's a problem, however."

"Sir?"

"The site has an old building, of no significant historical value, but an old building nonetheless. There's a stubborn tenant, a traditionalist, who believes the building should be safeguarded, even at the expense of progress."

Ponsonby paused, and Adrian knew he was supposed to speak—make an observation or ask an intelligent question. "Does the tenant actually own the building, or does it belong to someone else?"

"An excellent question," Ponsonby commended him. "He doesn't own it, but is essentially the authority over it by virtue of his job. He's responsible, and his employers recognize his authority. Unless, of course, something happens to diminish his standing with them, or other extenuating circumstances arise."

"You haven't been able to persuade him of the benefits of a Superstore—of how a Superstore will help the local economy?" Adrian's voice was not his own. The question was unlike any he thought he was capable of asking.

"No," Ponsonby replied. He spoke as if trying to be terribly diplomatic. "The tenant is simply . . . unreasonable."

"Unreasonable," Adrian echoed thoughtfully. "He likes the place that much?"

Ponsonby shook his head as if he were truly bewildered. "That's what I find the most astonishing about it! The tenant doesn't even like it where he is. He's miserable, if the truth be told.

I'd wager his family isn't happy there, either. Funny how some people cling to the very thing that is the source of their troubles. Now, what can we do that will help him—and help us?"

Adrian tensed as the game they were playing became clearer. He stared at the maps on the desktop as his mind raced. It was his move in this verbal chess game, and he had to make it carefully. "You'd have to give him a way out that will leave him with a sense of dignity. If he gives up the building, he'll have to do it with nothing to be ashamed of. He must have somewhere to go, a better position elsewhere, if you catch my meaning."

"An excellent point," Ponsonby nodded.

Adrian added for emphasis. "It's very important that he be taken care of properly."

"That can be arranged. But as I've said, he doesn't want to go. He won't be persuaded. He's unreasonable. How do we get him out and still leave him with a sense of dignity?"

Adrian turned away. He stood at one of the large windows looking out at the patio. Once again the move was his. Perhaps it was the most important move of all. But once it was made, there was no going back.

Ponsonby stood at Adrian's shoulder. "You've grown a lot since you came to work for me. I can see it already. You're not some spotty-faced loser. You have potential. You're worth all the time and energy I've put into you. Talk to me, Adrian. How do we do it?"

Adrian's cheeks flushed. He didn't want to lose the game now. It had become too important. He had to think like Ponsonby. That's what would it take to ease the nervous twinge in his heart.

They were talking about Christ Church, there was no doubt about it. And Ponsonby had hit the right chord when he had mentioned how miserable his father and the entire family were. It reverberated through all the questions Adrian himself had entertained. Why was his father so determined to hold on to the church? What purpose did it serve, except to keep him under the thumbs of the archdeacon and the bishop? *What was the point?*

Wouldn't escape be better? Wouldn't it help everyone concerned if Ponsonby could win and build his blasted Superstore? Perhaps if they were all forced to go somewhere else, they could salvage what was left of their relationships.

Adrian turned to Ponsonby. "We need to discover an angle, a bit of information, something that will completely and legally take the decision out of the tenant's hands," he said.

"For example?"

He didn't want to give too much away. "You say it's an old building. What kind of old building?"

"Why? What does that matter?"

"Because an old building may have structural problems that cause safety hazards."

Ponsonby smiled again. "You're on the right track, son."

The *son* gave Adrian a momentary pause, but he went on. "Look for sinking foundations or debris falling from the roof. If you could have the building inspected and show that it's a safety hazard, it would be closed down. If it's a terribly old building and the tenant isn't wealthy, renovations will be too expensive for him to accomplish."

"Of course," Ponsonby smiled. "It makes perfect sense."

Clydesdale spoke for the first time, cleaning his gold-wire spectacles as he did. "A battle over the building is the best way to go," he said in a thick, cultured voice. "That gives us a chance."

Ponsonby clapped Adrian on the back. "Well done, son, well done. The only thing left is for you to tell us what, precisely, is wrong with your father's church so we can call inspectors in to investigate. Is what you said true? Are the church foundations in trouble?"

Adrian couldn't look at Ponsonby, but fixed his eyes on a spot of green on one of the maps. "Well, the church is very old. It's reasonable to think that a church that old might have problems with its foundation. Maybe it's cracking and slipping. It might even be sinking. But I'm not an inspector. I'm just a kid. What do I know?"

Ponsonby sighed. "Right. Mr. Clydesdale, will you find out

when the church was last properly inspected? Not for a long time, I would suppose. Then I assume you could persuade our local council to grant permission for an inspection? As soon as possible? Tomorrow morning?"

"It won't be a problem," Clydesdale said.

Deep inside, Adrian felt the sense of release one has when a move has been made that cannot be reversed. Everything was set into motion. He clung to the notion that this would lead to nothing but good. His father would be freed from a dead-end job in a dead-end church. It would be best for everyone. All the same, he felt a little uneasy.

"Excellent. Thank you, Clydesdale." Ponsonby smiled. "And thank *you*, Adrian. You've proved my confidence in you. And for that, I want you to go to York with Lewis to represent me on a bit of business there."

"Represent you?"

"Yes, I have a store that's doing poorly. I want you to go in and check out the situation for me. Find out what's wrong. Make sure the managers are doing their jobs. Give me your impressions about how to salvage the store, improve its profit margin. You're a sharp lad. I trust you."

"Thank you, Mr. Ponsonby."

Ponsonby nodded. "You're welcome. Pack an overnight bag; Lewis will take you immediately."

"Immediately!"

"Yes, if you leave now, you'll be there this afternoon. I'll expect you back sometime tomorrow evening."

With the purposeful stride of someone on a great mission, Adrian headed for the door. Then he stopped and turned. "May I call my parents first?"

"I'll take care of that," Ponsonby said. "You just go."

Adrian went. He felt elated and free in that reckless way a child feels when he has thrown himself from a great height into the arms of someone dependable. Mr. Ponsonby would catch him. Mr. Ponsonby would take care of everything.

CHAPTER 20

Once they were pointed west for Bristol, the England Jeff had expected to see unfolded before him. Clusters of sun-washed villages nestled on rolling green hills, and rich farmland appeared and disappeared beyond the scratched windows of the bus. The tourist map in his lap gave villages names like Wootton Bassett, Tormarton, Chiseldon, and Pucklechurch. But it was hard for Jeff to appreciate his journey. His mind kept going back to Uncle Malcolm.

Arthur, meanwhile, had the look of a man who'd returned home after a long trip only to find that someone had built a factory on his playground.

They reached the city of Bristol in a little over two hours. The bus entered along a main highway that led into a labyrinth of streets to the city center, crowded with buildings old and new. Fancifully florid Victorian churches sat side by side with unimaginative concrete block buildings put up after World War II. The clouds had turned so gray that Jeff couldn't tell where the buildings ended and the sky began.

"Bristol is the largest city in southwest England," the bus driver's voice crackled through a distorted sound system. "During the Middle Ages, it was a textile center.

"Situated on the Avon River, about seven miles from the Bristol Channel, it is now a major seaport and an international finance center, second only to London. Bristol is known for exporting nuclear machinery, aircraft parts, tobacco, and food products."

On a large oblong stretch labeled St. Augustine's Parade but simply called "The Centre," the bus hugged a curb and stopped in front of a concert hall called The Hippodrome.

Arthur stood up, but Jeff nervously blocked his way to the aisle. "We have to stay together." Jeff gestured in as forceful a manner as one could with a man Arthur's size.

Arthur simply smiled at him. They stepped off the bus.

"I have to find a pay phone," Jeff said and scanned the area.

He spotted one and turned to tell Arthur to come with him. Arthur wasn't there. Jeff pivoted and quickly spied Arthur moving through the crowd down the street.

"Oh no," Jeff groaned and chased after him.

There are times when life really is like a movie, Jeff thought as he hustled through the crowd. In a strange city in a foreign country, he suddenly felt like an actor—no, a secret agent—shadowing his nemesis. Jeff ducked and dodged to keep Arthur in view. An easy task considering Arthur's size, but made difficult by the pedestrians and traffic crossing Denmark Street.

"Arthur!" Jeff wanted to cry out. But he knew it would be useless. Besides, secret agents don't call out the names of their prey.

What's he doing? Jeff wondered with exasperation. *Where does he think he's going? Doesn't he know that he's lost? Doesn't he know he needs me?* They were now headed up Park Street.

Jeff rounded the corner and nearly slammed into Arthur, who had stopped to look at two derelicts curled up on a bed of rags and whisky bottles. Arthur knelt next to one and poked gently at the threadbare coat. A tangled mass of hair and leatherlike skin lifted up to look at Arthur through slitted eyes.

Arthur said something softly to him.

The derelict, who didn't understand Latin and probably assumed he was being harassed, spat and hit Arthur full in the face. Then he lowered his head and went back to sleep.

Arthur slowly stood, wiping the spittle from his cheek. He looked at Jeff with an expression of immeasurable sadness. Then he gestured with both hands toward the derelicts and then the city. If Jeff had to interpret, it looked like a plea. "What has happened here? How can you have people sleeping on the street with all these buildings around?"

Jeff didn't have an answer for him. Remembering the task at hand, he grabbed Arthur's arm. "We have to go call Uncle Malcolm," he said, balling up his fist and putting it next to his head as if it were a telephone receiver.

Arthur looked at him quizzically, then spun around and

walked on up the street. Jeff gritted his teeth and followed along. *How do you communicate with someone who won't be spoken to?*

Arthur slowed his pace, as if he realized he didn't have to worry about escaping from Jeff. He strolled casually up the steep incline, scrutinizing the shops with their window displays. Jeff kept an eye out for a phone, but despaired of finding a way to restrain Arthur long enough to use one.

As they walked, Jeff also noticed that Arthur seemed to look intently into the faces of the people he passed. Some of them responded to his direct eye contact with uncomfortable expressions and annoyance. Once or twice, they recoiled so severely that they almost stumbled from the sidewalk into the street.

"Don't do that!" Jeff whispered harshly when one woman looked as if she might call the police.

Arthur cocked a furry eyebrow at him and smiled.

Jeff suddenly had a nagging sense that, for the first time since Arthur arrived in their time, he wasn't simply reacting to his circumstances. Arthur knew what he was doing.

Because Jeff was watching Arthur so closely, he didn't notice that the traffic on Park Street had dissipated. It was as if someone had turned the tap off, and now the last few drops—a couple of cars and vans—slid by.

At the top of the street, Arthur stopped to gaze curiously at a large Gothic building with a square bell tower. Winded now, Jeff tugged at Arthur's sleeve and made gestures and sounds that he hoped would communicate that they needed to stop for a minute, to rest.

Arthur seemed to understand—and maybe they both would have found a place to sit down—but Jeff noticed several policemen standing next to their white-and-blue cars near a museum and art gallery. Barriers had been put up at the intersection. If he'd known anything about British policemen, Jeff would have realized that the men weren't in their normal clothes, but were wearing riot gear. He had just thought how odd they looked and wondered why so many of them should be assembled, when suddenly a dam broke and a river of people washed out from the top of the street, through the buildings and alleyways, and rushed toward them.

Jeff looked around wildly, not sure of what he was seeing. It was as if a whistle had blown, and everyone in the area poured out of the buildings for a break. There were hundreds of them, some carrying placards and signs. As they drew closer, Jeff realized that the crowd was made up mostly of young faces.

The biggest crowds he had ever seen were Fawlt Line folks gathered for the homecoming football game with arch rival Hancock. This crowd made him nervous. This was a protest—a protest that was about to sweep them along in its current.

Arthur stood with his hands on his hips, like a man daring the tide to come in. The protesters, with shouts and chants, marched toward them, oblivious. Jeff pushed Arthur toward one side, but he wasn't interested in getting out of the way. The marchers surrounded them, and with the sheer force of their numbers carried them back down Park Street.

The signs and placards complained about students' rights being robbed and animal rights being abused and women's rights being thwarted, and Jeff knew that this wasn't a protest against one single problem, but against every problem the students could think of. Finally Jeff shouted at a young bearded, bespectacled man next to him. "What's going on? Why is everybody protesting?"

"The prince," the young man answered. "He's making a speech at the Council House. We want him to know we don't like the way the royalty live off the backs of the oppressed." He shouted for good measure, "Down with the monarchy!"

Several others picked up the chant, repeating it again and again.

Jeff glanced at King Arthur warily, glad he didn't understand what kind of protest he'd joined.

"We have to get out of here!" Jeff shouted at Arthur, who was looking around at the students with deep interest. He gave no sign that he understood or that he was inclined to go anywhere.

Again, Jeff felt he had been dropped into a scene from a movie.

Only now he wasn't a secret agent, but a helpless supporting character in an absurd comedy. He imagined the camera's point of view from somewhere high above them—a helicopter shot.

The camera pans across hundreds and hundreds of angry students marching down a street. Slowly the camera moves down to give a closer perspective on two characters in the middle of the crowd. We see a worried looking sixteen year old and an older, long-haired, bearded man with an inquisitive expression. Cut to: a close-up of the sixteen year old as he screams, "Help, Uncle Malcolm, help!" and then gets swallowed alive in the mass of humanity.

Back at the bottom of Park Street, the multitude broke out onto College Green, an expanse of lawn leading to the Council House grounds. The "House" itself was a massive, block-long crescent-shaped building with a moat and majestic fountains. On one side, a portable stage had been set up for the prince's speech. The police and security personnel watched the approaching throng apprehensively as they collected around the podium with those who'd already arrived for the event. Everyone pressed in close.

Jeff broke out in a sweat, trying to keep one eye on Arthur and the other on his own toes. Words were loudly exchanged between those who supported the prince and those who didn't. More chanting and sign-waving ensued. Jeff had a tight-throated feeling that anything could happen in this electric atmosphere.

Suddenly a roar went up from the crowd as a group of men in suits mounted the makeshift stand. A gray-headed, distinguished-looking gentleman approached the microphone and tried to speak above the shouts and jeers. He might have been a dean or a chancellor. Whoever it was, Jeff had a vague sense that the man was trying to establish some sense of propriety before introducing the prince. It didn't seem to work. He returned to the rest of the men—one of whom must've been the prince himself, Jeff figured—and they consulted, talking with pointed fingers and shaking heads. Finally a tall, brown-haired man stepped out from the consultation and moved to the microphone. It was the prince, and the crowd screamed blessings and curses.

Much later Jeff would think about stories throughout history where the catalyst for a major event turned out to be a single word or a little nudge or an unkind expression. Who fired the first shot at Lexington? What triggered the riot on the Bastille that led to the French Revolution? Who gave the fatal signal at Fort Sumter? And, finally, who started the riot on that gray day in Bristol?

Jeff would never know. What he did know was that the student protesters suddenly became a student mob, and everyone went collectively insane. Factions turned on each other with flying fists and thrown debris. People pushed, shoved, and trampled their way across the green and toward the podium. The prince and his entourage quickly left and disappeared into the council building. Police whistles blew and sirens wailed.

Jeff grabbed at Arthur's arm and, this time, he cooperated. With all the gentleness of a battering ram, Arthur pushed his way across the lawn toward an area that seemed deserted. It led to a small street, where they jogged left and followed it around to the rear of the building, away from the noise and violence. The two of them raced on, not sure where they were going, but wanting to distance themselves as far from the riot as possible. Jeff wondered if ducking into a back door might be the best way to go and gestured toward one. Arthur nodded and they went past a row of official-looking black cars, reaching the door just as it flew open.

What happened next took no more than a few seconds. But in this absurd film in which Jeff had found himself, everything shifted into slow motion, and a few seconds became minutes.

Two security men stepped through the door and, seeing only Jeff and Arthur, tried with only moderate success to push them aside. Jeff, of course, was no problem, and fell back easily.

The black cars, Jeff thought as he hit the ground, *they're headed for the black cars*.

Arthur stood like a brick wall, but it didn't matter to the security men. The move to the cars, like a football play after the ball has been hiked, was in motion and couldn't be stopped. The prince emerged through the door behind them. He walked confidently but quickly past Arthur and his prone sidekick.

Jeff wasn't sure whether Arthur actually said anything to the prince to get his attention. For whatever reason, though, the prince suddenly turned back toward Arthur, and they made eye contact. Arthur didn't move, nor even tried to speak, but the prince's expression suddenly changed. It was as if he had somehow recognized Arthur. His face seemed to say, "Oh, it's *you*."

Arthur's expression, on the other hand, was transformed into one of sadness and sympathy and he spoke to the prince in Latin.

The prince tilted his head curiously, pleasantly surprised. There was something about his look that conveyed appreciation to Arthur. The prince opened his mouth to speak, but the security agents misjudged the exchange between the two men, interpreting it as a threat to the prince's person. One threw a hard blow at Arthur's stomach, which only annoyed Arthur, while the other grabbed the prince and dragged him to a car. Arthur grabbed the security man and lifted him up off the ground by his lapels. What Arthur intended to do with him wasn't seen, since a third security man—a policeman—gave him a good thump on the back of the head with a baton.

On the ground together, Jeff sat up and Arthur rubbed his head as the engines revved and the cars squealed away down the street.

The crowd spilled around both sides of the building, and rocks and bottles were thrown angrily at the retreating vehicles. Jeff and Arthur got to their feet, sure once again that they were in the wrong place at the wrong time. Jeff looked around for a way to escape. As he turned, a bottle, launched by a student with exceptionally poor aim, flew missilelike toward him. He caught sight of it out of the corner of his eye and ducked—too late. It made a solid connection with the side of his head. A burst of light shattered into tiny pinwheels that spun into oblivion like Fourth of July fireworks.

The camera's point of view goes sideways and down.

Fade to black.

CHAPTER 21

Sirens wailed outside somewhere, but they didn't compare to the scream inside Jeff's head. He opened his eyes cautiously. He was in an office, stretched out on a lime green sofa he found so offensive he closed his eyes again. He gently eased himself up with a groan and lightly touched the bump where the bottle had hit.

"Easy now," a woman said. She was in a chair next to the sofa and peered over her reading glasses at him. Her milky white face and small blue eyes were crowned with a bush of silver hair. Jeff's immediate impression was that she looked like a librarian.

"Ow. Where am I?" Jeff asked.

"The Old Library."

His impression was right. Jeff swung his legs off the sofa. A dull pain shot through his head.

"Now, not so fast. That's quite a lump you have there," the woman said. "Caught in the riot, were you? A terrible mess. I rang for an ambulance, oh, must've been twenty minutes ago, but they haven't arrived. Probably won't. Worse cases than your bump to deal with, I suppose. Still, I think the police have it under control now."

"Where is he?"

"The man who brought you in? Your father?" she asked.

"He's not my father. He's . . . a friend," Jeff answered.

"He left."

"What?!?" Jeff exclaimed, to his regret. "Owwww!"

"Now just stay still," she advised.

Jeff spoke more softly. "He's gone?"

"Yes," she said sharply. Her tone and expression made Jeff think that she wanted to say more than that. He waited a moment. She continued with diplomatic effort. "He has a lot to learn about manners, that's certain. First he brought you in here and demanded that you be taken care of. Of course, I was only too happy to be of service and found ice for your lump until medical help could arrive. But then he started lecturing me about the condition of our country: people sleeping in the streets, riots by our young people, monarchs who are stripped of their power and helpless to—"

Jeff held up a hand. "Wait a minute. I'm sorry. He said all of that? In English?"

"No, not in English. In Latin."

"You know Latin?"

"I should say so. I went to Cambridge! Of course, I thought it was a bit peculiar that he insisted on speaking in Latin. I assumed he was a professor playing a game with me, but he persisted and—"

"But what happened to him? Please. You have to tell me everything he said."

She sighed impatiently. "I was telling you. He ranted and raved like a mad man. He blamed me personally for the trouble in this country. He said it was quite obvious that it was the teachings of the universities that have led to the decay he's observed. Of all the nerve."

Jeff's head throbbed harder, in time with his confusion. "The teachings of the universities? How does he know what you teach?"

"By asking, of course," she said, as if that answered everything. "As I said, when he first came in, carrying you and speaking proficient Latin, I assumed he was one of our professors. While I put an ice pack on your head, we chatted about the university. It was all quite cordial. He seemed fascinated by the scope of learning here."

Jeff thought back to Arthur on the street, looking at the shops and buildings, studying the faces of the people. *The walk wasn't some kind of impulsive event. There was method to his madness*, Jeff realized. *He was taking it all in. He was on a fact-finding tour to figure out what had become of his England.* Jeff considered Arthur with a new appreciation. Until that moment, he'd thought of Arthur as a big, uncivilized brute who'd probably become king by sheer strength and not through any inherent cleverness. But now . . .

"He was perfectly fine until we began to discuss religion," the librarian said.

"Religion?"

"He asked to see the bishop," she said. "It was obvious that he assumed a bishop or other cleric ran the university. When I informed him that the church had nothing to do with our university, he was quite shocked. I told him that we no longer require our instructors to believe in God or Jesus Christ. Then he simply lost control. He said that such faithlessness is always at the heart of a nation's downfall—and it often begins with apostate teachers. Honestly, I feared he might resort to physical violence. He said he'd banish us all if he could."

Jeff scrubbed his hands over his face to hide his smile.

"Is he some sort of fundamentalist?" she asked.

"In a way, I guess," Jeff replied.

"He said over and over that it was the fulfillment of prophecy. The bishop was right. The country had been left to godless pagans. To what bishop was he referring?"

"I don't know."

"It was the most remarkable thing," she said, shaking her head so that her loose jowls dangled. "Where did he learn his Latin? It was authentically ancient."

"He didn't mention who he was?"

"I asked, but he ignored the question. That's when he left. He asked me to take care of you, and simply walked out. Not even a word of thanks," she said indignantly.

"Well, thank you from me." Jeff smiled, and another flicker of pain reminded him of his wound.

"You're most welcome," she said.

"He didn't say anything about where he was going?"

"Not a peep," she answered, "You're an American, I assume."

"Yes, ma'am," Jeff answered and wondered what made her ask at this particular moment.

"Is this your first visit to England?"

"Yeah," he said. "We flew in this morning."

"Quite an introduction—arriving for a riot like that."

Jeff nodded agreeably. "It's definitely not in the tour books."

"Well . . ." She suddenly stood up. "You seem to be quite recovered. If there's anything further I can do, don't hesitate to ask. Otherwise, I must return to my duties. I believe the police have the crowds under control, if you wish to leave."

On rubbery legs, Jeff also stood. "There is one thing, if you wouldn't mind.

"Yes?" she asked with a cautionary tone.

"May I use your phone? There's somebody I have to call right away."

Finding Uncle Malcolm was no easy task. Jeff couldn't remember the name of the hotel near the airport nor imagine what Uncle Malcolm might have done after he realized that Jeff and Arthur were gone. Would he go to the hotel and wait, or try to find them? Even using the telephone was a chore. The phone numbers for information and the operator weren't the same as in America. Finally, after cross-referencing a telephone book for the umpteenth time, Jeff settled on the most obvious course of action: call Mrs. Packer.

Across the transatlantic lines, her relief was audible. "Your uncle is beside himself with worry. He couldn't imagine how to find you. And then he heard about the riots there. "

"He knew we went to Bristol?"

"Someone saw you get on the bus," she said.

"Where's Uncle Malcolm now?" Jeff asked.

"At a hotel there in the—what do you call it?—city center. Probably not far from where you are now."

Thank God, Jeff thought. *He's nearby.*

"He had hoped you'd have the presence of mind to call me," Mrs. Packer said, pleased to be Operation Central in this crisis.

Jeff tried to keep the conversation on track. "Which hotel?"

"The Royal," she replied.

"Thanks, Mrs. Packer," Jeff said and hung up.

The librarian knew where the Royal Hotel was and gave Jeff explicit directions. Ten minutes later, he stepped into the thick red-velvet-and-gold-lined reception area. A crystal chandelier twinkled high above him. A thin-mustached desk manager eyed him suspiciously. Four minutes and three floors after that, Jeff was being embraced by Uncle Malcolm in his hotel room.

"What a nightmare! The two of you gone, the riots . . ." After letting go of Jeff, Uncle Malcolm looked anxiously at the doorway and hallway beyond. "Where's Arthur?"

Jeff grimaced. "The nightmare isn't over. Arthur left, and I don't know where he went."

Malcolm's face fell. "Oh, no."

"But," Jeff went on, "strange as it sounds, I think *he* knew where he was going."

Malcolm looked at Jeff inquisitively. "What do you mean?"

"I mean . . . I think I should tell you everything that's happened since we got on that bus."

CHAPTER 22

On a thick bed of grass in the middle of a Somerset field, King Arthur folded his arms behind his head and looked up at the moon. It stared mutely back with its unblinking eye. Arthur didn't mind. He and the moon had been friends for a long time. And on this cool, clear night when Arthur was too exhausted from walking to go to sleep, he looked to his old friend to comfort him. What else did he have?

The day had been a long one. Not because he had walked so many miles—he was a soldier and used to that—but because of the mind-numbing, horrific vision of the future he had seen. Arthur was not a superstitious man, yet he was frightened in an indescribable way. He was scared by the endless gray stone structures that housed the thousands and thousands of people, crammed and congested, their faces reflecting an inner emptiness. Merlin had taught him well to understand the hearts of men, their hunger and need, for it would help him to be a wise and benevolent king. In the great city he had left a few hours before, the hearts he saw were cold and empty. If they contained anything at all it was a silent scream of buried pain, of yearning that could never be satisfied by outward means, of hope choked by despair. The mob's riot and the lost and confused expression of the prince confirmed it. For all of their monumental structures, self-propelling carts, and mechanical birds, they were spirits in bondage.

"For what do they gain if they possess the entire world but lose their own souls?" our Savior had once asked.

Arthur knew the answer. For he himself had possessed Camelot, that world of all worlds, and lost it to those of unfaithful hearts and wicked desires. The Grail was taken away from him and would not be regained. Not in his time. He knew that if he ever went back, it would be to face Mordred, that dark and monstrous reflection of himself—his own nephew by witchery. This future world seemed to be inhabited by hundreds of Mordreds.

Oh, God! he cried out at the unblinking moon as it stared him down like his own regret. *Why have you brought me here, unless it is to restore the Grail, to bring faith to these people, to drive out the faithless, to give them their own glimpse of Camelot? To what end would You show me these things, make me part of this terrible dream, if not to glorify You?*

No words came to him—from God or anyone else.

Still, he would carry on. He knew that much. If indeed there were a purpose to this living dream, he would find it further along in his journey. He wasn't sure how or why, but he would persevere. Like a siren song, his quest called to him, and he would follow—even if it meant his own destruction on the rocks. As a true knight, he had no choice. It was the brave and chivalrous thing to do. It was the Christian thing to do.

Arthur stared at the moon until its light was all he could see. It shone on him then as it did in his memories of a golden age, where he sat with valiant knights at a round table, by his side a beautiful queen, ruling an invincible kingdom. All because a boy had drawn a sword from a stone. Would the same happen again if the nation saw a similar miracle?

In wonder he drifted to sleep, the once and future king.

CHAPTER 13

Myrddin slid his mystical old bones into the second pew at Christ Church in Wellsbridge. It was early in the morning, and the church was empty. That suited Myrddin just fine. He enjoyed the unique silence of the ancient church when no one else was around. For him, it seemed to hum with the timeless prayers of God's people. A rosy-cheeked maiden from 1590, a harried soldier from 1817, a struggling smudged-faced miner from 1934—their whispered entreaties floated and mingled, drenching the cracked walls and bathing the stone altar in grace. Myrddin knelt, made the sign of the cross, and pressed his face against his gnarled, folded hands.

He prayed, "Glory be to the Father, and to the Son, and to the Holy Ghost . . ."

The thud of the door at the far end of the church startled him but, determined not to be distracted from his prayers, he continued. "As it was in the beginning, is now and ever shall be: world without end. Amen. Praise ye the Lord . . ."

Footsteps clicked against the stone floor and echoed throughout the church. Not one set, but several. Low voices mumbled to each other. Someone gave instructions, and the footsteps scattered in several directions around him.

Myrddin frowned but continued to pray. "O come, let us sing unto the Lord: let us heartily rejoice in the strength of our salvation . . ."

A familiar set of footsteps approached him, and an equally familiar hand rested on Myrddin's shoulder. He turned to look into the stricken face of Graham Peters.

"Myrddin," Graham whispered in a choked voice.

Myrddin knew before Graham said another word.

"The inspectors are here," said Graham. "They're going to close down the church."

Myrddin thrust his chin out. "Not until I've finished my prayers."

Graham started to protest. "But, Myrddin—"

"If you're the man I think you are, you'll kneel here with me and say your prayers too," he said. "They wouldn't dare interfere with morning prayers."

"They might," Graham said as he scooted in next to Myrddin.

"They might try," the old sage grunted.

To the annoyance of the three inspectors, Myrddin and Graham prayed for an hour. But they prayed without interruption.

Jeff lost count of the number of times they went over the story. All morning, they considered again and again every detail of what had happened since Arthur's arrival in the present time. Malcolm was certain that they would discover not only where he was headed, but why he was headed there. Jeff was too jet-lagged to think about it.

"We're missing something," Malcolm said as he peeked out of the bathroom. Half of his face was covered with shaving cream. "There's a link we haven't established. None of this has happened by chance."

Jeff pulled the blanket over his head. They'd been up late and, for him, it still felt early, even though the clock announced in bright red numbers that it was nine o'clock. His head still hurt. He was in a bad mood. "I don't care," he announced.

"From the very beginning, there's been something, something, something . . ." Malcolm mused on the word *something* several times as he disappeared back into the bathroom.

Under the covers, Jeff's mind clicked into gear against his will. He opened his eyes and looked deep into the cavelike darkness created by the folds of the bedcovers. *Something was missing. A link.* The phrase echoed around in his brain, like a lone voice in that cave he imagined. Jeff resisted the urge to explore the idea any further. He wanted to sleep. But the phrase continued to bounce around and, as sometimes happens with patterns of thought, the image of a cave turned into a dark ruin, like the ruin Uncle Malcolm had set up in his historical village. He remembered the last time he was there. He and Elizabeth had taken the sword and clothes to hide in the stone table. Both had disappeared.

Jeff threw the covers away from his head. So much had happened since then that he hadn't really thought about it before. "Did they slip back through a crack in time?" he wondered, then asked out loud.

Uncle Malcolm stuck his head out of the bathroom again. "What?"

"The sword and the clothes. Why did they disappear like that? Was it some kind of magic?"

"Don't be silly. Magic has nothing to do with this."

"Then what happened? Did they go back to Arthur's time?"

"Perhaps they did. If the church ruin is where the time fault somehow opened, then maybe it opened again to allow the sword and clothes to slip back through."

"Why?"

"How do I know why? Why is any of this happening? I don't know."

"But the church ruin is kind of at the center of all this, right? It's where Arthur woke up when he first got here. It's where he ran when he escaped from the hospital. It's where he told Alan to have us hide his stuff."

"Just say it, Jeff. What are you thinking?"

Jeff replied thoughtfully with another question. "Where did the church ruin come from?"

"Here in England, of course, but—" Malcolm stopped and came out of the bathroom in his T-shirt and jogging pants. "Wait a minute."

Jeff was ahead of him. "I know it's kinda crazy, but what if Arthur wasn't supposed to show up in Fawlt Line? What if the only reason he showed up there was because—"

"I moved the church ruin from here in England!"

"Yeah."

Malcolm slapped an open palm against his forehead. "Good

grief! Where has my brain been?"

Jeff sat up. "Where did the church ruin come from?"

Malcolm gestured toward the small writing desk in the corner of the room. "There's a road atlas on the desk. Take a look while I finish shaving. The ruin came from a tiny village called Wellsbridge. If I remember right, it's not far from here."

A moment later, Jeff had checked through the index and opened to the proper page number. "It looks like Wellsbridge is south, maybe southwest of here. Not very far," he called out.

Malcolm joined Jeff at the desk. "Where?"

"Right there." Jeff's finger followed a red line—an "A road"— from Bristol down to the tiny print that said Wellsbridge.

"Interesting," Malcolm said and tugged at his ear.

Jeff pondered the map. "It doesn't look very big. It's near— what's this town?—Glastonbury."

"Glastonbury!" Malcolm exclaimed.

"What's the matter?"

"Glastonbury is where Arthur was supposedly buried—or, if you believe the other legend, the Lady of the Lake transported his body in a mysterious ship to some kind of paradise."

Jeff drew an invisible circle on the map with his finger. "It's all in the same area."

"Then I guess we know where we have to go."

Jeff and Malcolm got dressed, packed up, checked out of the hotel, and climbed into the white Vauxhall in the parking garage. It was odd for Jeff to get in on the left-hand side and not face a steering wheel.

The sun drenched the city in a clear light that gave sharp definition to the buildings and blue sky. *No riots today,* Jeff thought as they passed Park Street and the university buildings. Apart from a few boarded-up windows, there was nothing to indicate that anything had happened the day before. *Maybe things will start to go right for a change.*

Malcolm eased the car through Bristol's midday traffic. He and Jeff were both oblivious to the small green car behind them that followed their every move.

"Sit down, sit down." The archdeacon gestured to Graham from behind his enormous oak desk. It was a familiar scene.

Graham declined the offer. "Neville—"

"Tea?"

Graham shook his head. "No, thank you."

"Just as well," he said. "Kettle's broken."

Graham shifted from one foot to another in agitation. This was the moment Graham had been dreading since he became vicar of Christ Church: demanding funds to rebuild his church. "Neville, we have to talk."

"We certainly do," the archdeacon said. "Imagine the embarrassing position in which I was placed to learn from a layman that your church has a crumbling foundation. It's scandalous. Did you, my fellow churchman, tell me? No. Why not?"

Graham was thrown by this sudden reversal. He stammered, "With respect, Neville, I did—or tried to. I've reported that the church was in dire straits."

"Forgive me," the archdeacon said without really wanting forgiveness. "The phrase 'dire straits' is a far cry from the extreme condition of Christ Church. The foundation is sinking, Graham. How could you let it happen?"

"I didn't *let* it happen, Neville," he said, frowning. How had this become his fault? And how did the archdeacon—and Ponsonby—find out about the church's foundation, anyway?

"I suppose you're here now to ask the bishop for money."

Graham leaned on the back of the velvety ornate guest chair for support. "Well, yes, I am. If we don't get repairs underway immediately, Ponsonby will use this as a means to build his Superstore."

"You have no one to blame but yourself if that happens," the archdeacon said sharply. "The bishop isn't pleased."

"If he isn't pleased, then he must appreciate the seriousness of the situation," Graham said.

The archdeacon fixed his gaze on Graham. "He appreciates it and is at a loss as to what should be done about it."

"Repairing the church is the obvious choice."

"Obvious to you, perhaps, but not to those who must manage the very limited funds of the church. With so many pressing needs, we simply can't see our way clear to invest a lot of money in a church with such a small congregation. Case closed, I'm afraid."

Graham was prepared for an argument, but not such a direct shutdown. It immediately brought him to one conclusion. "Ponsonby got to you, didn't he?"

"I beg your pardon?"

"Has he already made you an offer?"

The archdeacon frowned. "Be careful what you imply, Graham. Your situation isn't secure."

"Of course it isn't. It never has been." Sweat beaded on Graham's forehead as the simple truth dawned on him. He wanted to sit down but didn't, for fear that it might be construed as weakness. His mouth moved as the thoughts formed in his mind. "Moving me from Bristol to Wellsbridge was part of the plan, wasn't it? Move me to Christ Church and, when the time came, you could get rid of us both. Did you always know about the sinking foundation?"

The archdeacon rolled his eyes. "Don't be paranoid. You make it sound like a conspiracy. Next you'll be saying we shot J. F. K."

"This whole thing seems terribly convenient," Graham said in a dry, raspy voice.

"If it's convenient, it's only because you made it so. Your conduct—and your son's conduct—have contributed greatly to our present decision. If you were on this side of the desk you'd see that. Even if we had the money, which we don't, we'd be fools to pour it into Wellsbridge. It's a dead church! Why not sell the land to Ponsonby if he can use it? It'll certainly fund ministry opportunities elsewhere." It was an ironclad argument, and the archdeacon knew it.

"And if I raise the money for the repairs myself?"

The archdeacon smiled. "Then I'll give up everything they taught me in seminary and believe in miracles once again. You can't do it. Not in the amount of time we have."

"Which is?"

"Three days. That's as much as the bishop is willing to give for any appeal. He's leaving for Africa and wants the matter settled before he goes. If you want to save your little church, Graham, you have three days."

Graham walked into an empty kitchen and glanced guiltily at Christ Church through the window. He wanted to explain to the old building. He wanted to say that he'd been a pawn and didn't even realize it until it was too late. He wanted to confess that he had failed and then ask the church for absolution.

"Anne? Adrian?" he called out to the muffled silence. No answer. He was relieved. He wasn't up for explaining to his wife and son how badly he'd botched it—how the church would be torn down and he would be out of a job. Anne would be upset, but strong. Adrian would probably grin and say he knew all along it would end this way. Graham had been played for a fool. He could even imagine the conversation between Ponsonby and the archdeacon:

Where will we find a man who is so weak-minded and spineless that we'll be able to close down the church without a fuss?

Oh, I have just the man in Bristol. Graham Peters. He's a pushover. If we put him in there, it'll be no time at all before the circumstances will be perfect to make a move.

He kicked a chair angrily as the truth poured into his brain. Little wonder, then, that Adrian had rebelled. Little wonder that his son didn't respect him at all. He thought back to their conversations on the way home from the train station and when they worked together on the church. It was as if Adrian knew even then what was happening. Adrian saw what Graham refused to see. Out of the mouths of babes comes wisdom, the Scriptures said. How very true.

Graham leaned forward on the table. His eye caught the open newspaper spread out in front of him. Anne had written a note with an arrow pointing to one of the articles in the lower right-hand corner of the page. "Thought you'd be interested," her scribble said.

Graham looked at the article. ARTHUR ARRIVES IN ENGLAND, the headline shouted boldly. Underneath, a short piece said that a man calling himself Arthur Pendragon had arrived from America the previous morning at Heathrow. Investigation by the reporter revealed that he was the same Arthur who'd been knocked off of a horse in America several days before and had been arrested as a public nuisance. Details were sketchy about how he'd escaped from the mental ward where he had been detained, but apparently he'd gotten a passport and flown to England with two other persons of unknown identity. He was currently at large somewhere near Bristol. The Home Office said they would inquire into the legitimacy of his passport.

Myrddin will be interested, Graham thought. Then wryly he thought about how he and Myrddin would have all the time in the world to talk about Arthur, now that he was unemployed. He slumped into the chair dejectedly.

The back door opened, and Anne walked in. "Hello, darling," she said.

Graham grunted.

She carried two grocery bags, which she immediately deposited on the counter. She didn't bother to unpack them, turning to Graham instead. "I suppose the meeting with the archdeacon didn't go very well."

"It went very well indeed—if you're the archdeacon," Graham said.

"I'm sorry." She moved next to him and caressed the back of his head and neck. "Have you thought about what you might do?"

"I have to raise the money somehow if I'm going to save the church," he answered. "I suppose I could go door-to-door around Wellsbridge and ask my parishioners to help. That'll yield around eight pounds. Otherwise, I have no idea."

Anne slid into his lap as she used to when they were first married. She wrapped her arms around him. "Oh, Graham," she said sympathetically.

Graham couldn't look into her eyes. "I feel so foolish, Anne. I've been a complete and total sucker. Where am I going to come up with the kind of money we need to fix the church? How can I hope to battle Ponsonby on that level?"

Anne nuzzled her head against the curve of his shoulder. She spoke softly, "Maybe you can't. Maybe you shouldn't try to fight the way others fight."

"What do you mean?"

"I've been thinking about it all morning." She sighed, then sat up to face him again. "You're not terribly shrewd when it comes to politics."

"Thank you, my love."

"Be honest, Graham. It's not a game you play very well. It makes you nervous and sweaty. Which is precisely why a political machine like the archdeacon has been able to manipulate you so effectively."

Graham waited a moment. "Yes—and?"

"The same goes for money," she continued. "Ponsonby has all the money in the world. He lives it and breathes it. You don't. And to think that you'll be able to take him on that way . . . well, he'll hang you out to dry."

"Your confidence in me is overwhelming," Graham said. "So, if I can't battle this problem politically or financially, what's left?"

"You're a kindhearted *pastor*, Graham," she said softly and reasonably. "Fight with the thing you do know about. Fight it in the spiritual realm."

Graham laughed. "Spiritual? I'm sorry, but I don't see that the spiritual fits into this at all. This time it really is about money. The only way to stop Ponsonby is to fight on his terms. I'm not sure you understand what's at stake here."

"I understand perfectly what's at stake," Anne answered in her clipped, annoyed tone. "I don't believe my ears. Aren't you the one who always says that in every situation, the spiritual aspects are the most important ones to consider?"

Graham merely shook his head. "It's not so easy this time."

Anne slid from his lap and went to the counter to unload the grocery bags. "The church's foundation is slipping. Does that mean your foundation is slipping, too?"

Graham didn't answer. She had zeroed in on the heart of the problem, but he was helpless to respond.

She unpacked the bags with her back to him. "Darling, you're a man of faith . . . of prayer. There was a time when it used to shine from you as it did from no one I'd ever known. You believed in miracles. Where is your faith now? Is it in fighting the way Ponsonby fights—in believing that money is the only way out? Or is it somewhere else? *What do you believe, Graham?*"

He took his collar off and tossed it onto the table. "I believe in what I see. The politically and financially powerful are the ones who control everything."

"And a miracle?"

"Not likely," he said.

He looked out the window toward the church again. An overwhelming sense of guilt rushed back at him—not only for his failure to save the building, but for failing to muster the faith he knew he should have. What kind of miracle could he hope for now?

A tall man with long hair and a beard rounded the corner of the church tower. He seemed to be examining—or exploring—the church.

"I thought the city inspectors left," Graham said.

"They did."

Graham sighed. "Then I wonder who this character is."

Graham found the stranger poking around the site where the oldest part of the church had been. He was a large man. A Viking in a modern suit, Graham thought as he approached him. Something about him made Graham think he was a tourist. Wellsbridge got those every now and then, mostly when they'd gotten lost on their pilgrimage to Glastonbury. Catholics and Protestants alike came to worship at the Abbey ruin for its spiritually historic value. But others from Celtic and New Age practices came to soak up what they thought were magical "vibrations." This man looked as if he might fit in any of those categories.

"May I help you?" Graham asked.

Startled, the man turned to Graham and stood silently with his hands on his hips. He eyed Graham carefully as if he hoped to recognize him.

"The church is closed for repairs. I'm sorry for any inconvenience." Graham noticed that the man's clothes, though of nice quality, looked wrinkled and dirty. *Homeless*, he thought. *A derelict.*

The stranger smiled and, in a foreign language, asked Graham a question.

Graham was surprised. Like many people of his generation, he had had to learn Latin as part of his classical education. But it had been a long time since he heard anyone speak the language, and he certainly didn't expect it from this man. He translated the question slowly in his mind. *Why is the church locked?*

"I told you—" Graham began in English.

The stranger interrupted him with a disapproving wave. "Speak in my language," the man said.

Graham thought it was some kind of joke. How could his language be a dead language like Latin? Graham stammered, "All right. I'll have to speak slowly because I don't know Latin very well."

"As you wish."

"The church is closed," Graham explained. "It needs repairs to its foundations."

The stranger frowned. "What has become of this part of the church?"

Graham constructed the sentence in his mind, then carefully spoke. "It was dismantled and sold to someone in America."

The stranger nodded. "I have seen it."

Graham tensed. Either this was a joke, or the man was a few degrees short of a right angle. "Who sent you? Why are you here?"

The stranger reached into his jacket pocket and produced a colorful tourist's map. He unfolded it and pointed to Glastonbury.

"Glastonbury," Graham said. So he was a pilgrim.

"By what name is this town known?" the stranger asked.

"This is Wellsbridge," Graham answered, then pointed to where the name should have been on the map, but wasn't. The village was too insignificant.

The stranger folded the map up again and shoved it into his pocket. "It is a fine church and beautiful, priest. Do not lock it. It is the house of the most Holy God and should be open to all."

Graham smiled ironically. "Tell that to the inspectors."

The stranger looked at him curiously.

"Never mind," Graham said.

"I will return," the man said and walked away from the church in the direction of Glastonbury.

Graham watched him go. If his mind hadn't been on so many other things, he might have noticed the low hum emanating from the pile of stones and debris next to the wall of the church. He returned to his house to plan his strategy for battling Ponsonby.

CHAPTER 15

"Hi, Mum. It's me," Adrian said above the roar of traffic.

"Where are you?" Anne asked. Even at that distance, Adrian heard the stiffness in her voice.

"On the M5 near Droitwich, I think," he shouted down the phone. "I'm on my way back from York."

Silence. Then: "You haven't heard, I suppose."

"Heard what?"

"The church was overrun with inspectors this morning. They found out about the foundation. We're closed for the time being."

"Oh," Adrian said, his voice catching in his throat. Ponsonby worked faster than he'd thought possible.

"You're not surprised," his mom said.

Adrian tried to deflect her statement. "How did Dad react?"

"He went to see the archdeacon in hope of getting money for repairs. The archdeacon said no. It seems the site will be sold to Ponsonby, and your father will be out of work."

Adrian wasn't sure he'd heard right. "Out of work? They'll just send him to another church, right?"

Was it the phone line, or did his mother's voice go cold? "The archdeacon made it fairly clear that they won't."

"No! They wouldn't do that him!" Adrian cried out. There must be a mistake. He had an agreement with Ponsonby.

"Sorry, but I believe they would," she said. "No doubt you're pleased."

"Pleased?"

"Surely this justifies the lack of respect you have for your father. Your boss has won." Icicles formed on the line. "You made the right choice."

"Mum—" he began.

"Don't 'mum' me, Adrian," she snapped. "Maybe one day I'll understand you. But right now I don't and . . . and . . ." her voice faltered. Was she crying? "I believe this conversation is over."

The line clicked as she hung up.

Adrian leaned his forehead against the phone. Something had gone wrong. His dad was supposed to lose the church, not his *job*.

Lewis appeared at Adrian's side, "Well, lad?"

"I have to talk to Ponsonby," he growled.

Ponsonby was at his desk, clicking away on a computer keyboard. He barely looked up as Adrian entered his study. "Oh, good. You're back. How did it go in York?"

Adrian stood at the head of the desk. "I'm not here to talk about York. I want to talk to you about the church."

Ponsonby pushed himself away from the keyboard. He slumped into his chair, his hands folded calmly across his chest. "You heard. Too bad. I wanted to tell you the good news myself."

"Good news!"

"Of course," Ponsonby smiled. "We should have this deal sewn up in no more than three days."

Adrian struggled against Ponsonby's self-assurance. "But what about my dad?"

"What about him?"

"He thinks he's out of a job," Adrian explained. "He says they won't assign him to another church."

Ponsonby looked concerned. "Really? That's too bad."

Adrian cleared his throat. He needed to be calm. "Mr. Ponsonby, it was my understanding that you would arrange with the archdeacon for my father's transfer to another church."

"Where on earth did you get that idea?" Ponsonby asked, incredulous.

"From our meeting. When I told you about the church."

Ponsonby shook his head. "I'm sorry, Adrian, but you had the wrong understanding."

"No, sir," Adrian said firmly. "I didn't have the wrong understanding. You were going to take care of my father."

Ponsonby spread his arms. "Who do you think I am, the Archbishop of Canterbury?"

"It was part of the deal. You got what you needed to close the church, providing my father was taken care of. We stood right here and you agreed. You lied to me."

Ponsonby sat up sharply as if he might fly out of the chair and into Adrian's face. "I did not lie, Adrian."

"You have another name for it, then?" Adrian asked.

This time Ponsonby did come out of his chair, but not at Adrian. He turned to the large French windows. "I didn't want to have to tell you, but I will to save my own name. I talked to the archdeacon about your father, and he adamantly refused to transfer him to another church."

"Why?"

"Your father isn't wanted anymore," Ponsonby stated. "They've been planning his dismissal for a long time."

"No!" Adrian cried out.

Ponsonby turned to face Adrian. "You must understand something about your father. He may be great with people, but he's awful at the things that really count in our society."

"Like what?"

"Maneuvering, back-scratching, and making the right friends."

"You mean church politics," Adrian said as if the words were made of poison. "Is that what this is all about? Church politics?"

"Yes. And the sooner your father realizes it the better," Ponsonby asserted. "Why are you so surprised? Didn't our time together teach you anything? We talked about people like your father. They don't survive in our world."

"What happens to them?"

Ponsonby shrugged. "Frankly, I have no idea. I don't keep company with people like your father very much." Ponsonby leaned toward him. "Listen carefully, boy. I don't keep company with people like your father. Do you get my meaning?"

Adrian did.

"You have a choice to make about what you believe in—and that choice will guide you into the future. Are you following your father down his path, or me down mine?"

CHAPTER 16

"Your wife is right, you know," Myrddin said to Graham as he poured their tea.

"I thought you'd say that."

Myrddin sat down across from him. "All our battles are spiritual in nature. This one included." He smiled, "Though I suspect it's not the battle you think it is."

Graham looked at him. "I'm trying to save Christ Church."

"Are you? Why?"

"Because it's . . . it's worth saving," Graham said.

"Why?"

Graham thought a moment. "It's a good church, beautiful in its way. The people of Wellsbridge deserve their own church."

Myrddin leaned forward and rested his elbows on the creaky wood table. "I don't believe you. This isn't about a building."

"Isn't it? Why not?" Graham asked.

"Because it's an average church in appearance, not historically significant in an obvious way, and most of the churchgoing people in Wellsbridge would be just as happy attending church at Glastonbury or Wells."

"You're not terribly encouraging."

"I'm trying to discern your heart, Graham. Why do you want to save the church so badly?"

Graham closed his eyes wearily. Why was he here with this old man instead of out trying to raise money? "Because it . . . it'll save my job."

"So this is merely an exercise to maintain your vocation?"

"No," Graham said impatiently. "It's more than that. If I save the church, I'll save . . . myself."

"Yourself."

They looked at each other in silence as a clock ticked on the mantle. Graham wasn't sure how far he wanted to go. It had been a day of revelations, and he wasn't sure he could take anymore.

But he knew Myrddin wouldn't let him off with easy answers. Confess and get it over with, he decided.

"I think Anne hit the nail on the head when she said that the church's foundation was crumbling and so was mine. She asked me what I believe, Myrddin, and I couldn't answer her. My foundation is in a sorry state. And somehow it seems that . . . if I can restore the church, then maybe I'll feel restored too." It sounded stupid to his ears. Graham waited for Myrddin's verdict.

Myrddin smiled. "Now we're getting closer to the truth. How do you propose to save the church and yourself? By spending the next three days trying to raise money that no one you know has?"

"If that's what it takes," Graham said.

"And will that save you or merely reinforce what you already cynically believe?"

"Eh?"

"You've picked up the confused notion that money and power are the only ways to survive in this world."

"Experience can be a great teacher," Graham said sarcastically.

"A great teacher, but a rotten god."

"What?"

Myrddin rephrased his statement. "By all means, be taught by experience, but not to the exclusion of the power of God. Things are happening, Graham. We're on the edge of a wondrous time."

Graham desperately wanted to believe him. To believe in wonders, in miracles, would be marvelous.

"Did you see the article in the paper?" Myrddin asked.

Graham frowned as his hope of wonders and miracles crashed against the rocks of Myrddin's obsession with Arthur. "Yes."

"Arthur's here."

Graham groaned. "It's a tabloid article, Myrddin. Last week they said aliens had kidnapped the prime minister's brain."

"Ah, but this is true."

"How do you know?"

"I can feel it. He's here." Myrddin's eyes were wide with awe.

Graham thought then as he had before, that if he weren't so

close to the old man, he'd write him off as mad. He chose his words carefully. "Myrddin, forgive me. You had me going for a minute there. But I can't believe in this nonsense about Arthur. If you're trying to make a connection between my struggling faith and the arrival of a mythological king, don't bother. It won't happen. It can't happen."

"And you're the wise sage who is going to tell God what He can or cannot do? *Est autem fides credere quod nondum vides; cuius fidei merces est videre quod credis!*" he shouted.

Faith is to believe what you do not see; the reward of this faith is to see what you believe, Graham translated. The Latin made him think of the stranger at the church. "Why is everyone speaking Latin at me today?"

"You've persuaded yourself to believe in money and power, so that's all you see. But you can see so much more if you'll see with your faith. Perhaps if you—" Myrddin broke off mid-sentence. "Who's been speaking to you in Latin?"

"Just a traveler who stopped by the church. Homeless, I thought, except that he insisted that we speak in Latin. Awfully peculiar. He was on his way to Glastonbury."

"Glastonbury," Myrddin mused.

Graham decided to get things back on track so he could leave. "Look, Myrddin, everything you say sounds good, but to me your words seem idealistic. I don't know how to make them work in this situation."

Myrddin half-smiled as he stood up. "You want to see how? Come walk with me."

Graham declined. "I don't have time. I have to call a meeting of the church committee."

"The committee will wait. Walk with me. If not for the sake of your soul, then come for the sake of our friendship."

"You're a strange old mystic," Graham said affectionately. "Why should I?"

Myrddin placed a hand on his shoulder. "To see with your eyes what your lack of faith won't let you see."

Arthur, son of Uther and Igraine, apprentice to Merlin, and legendary King of Britain, entered Glastonbury with a heavy heart and weary legs just as the clouds gathered for a major downpour. Never had he felt more tired or alone. The constant assault of unfamiliar sights and times, a strange language, and an uncertain mission bore down on him. Worse were the moments when he thought he had recognized an area of land, only to find it marred with black roads, houses, and buildings.

Glastonbury brought the most mixed feelings of all. It had once been a beautiful settlement village on an island called Avalon. Arthur knew it well.

Avalon was the cradle of Christianity in Britain. Joseph of Arimathea, Arthur's direct ancestor and the man who owned the tomb Jesus Christ had been buried in, had traveled there with eleven disciples in the first century to spread the Gospel of Christ. He had brought with him the chalice used by Jesus at the last supper before His crucifixion and resurrection.

The story was told that one Christmas morning, Joseph wearily sat down and stuck his staff into the ground. It sprouted and blossomed into a hawthorn bush. He and his disciples interpreted it to mean that they were to stop their journeying and build a church there dedicated to the chalice. Years later, Arthur himself had worshiped at the church, often at Christmas when the bush flowered in memory of the birth of Jesus.

More recently (at least to Arthur), it was also the site where the evil Melwas had kidnapped Queen Guinevere, Arthur's wife. Arthur laid siege to the castle and, had it not been for the compassionate intercessions of that great man of God, Gildas, the end would have been spilled blood and painful death. But Guinevere was freed without harm. Arthur smiled to remember that, later, Lancelot had a conflict with Melwas and killed him in single combat. Justice had been served after all.

But now all was different. Avalon the island had been replaced by Glastonbury the town. Arthur struggled to identify what was left. From the point where he first approached the town, he saw Tor Hill. Like everything else, it had changed. Tor Hill now had a stone tower on top. When it had been built or why was more than Arthur could guess.

Arthur walked along a road that took him deeper into congested traffic and crowds of tourists. He felt uncomfortable and out of place in the middle of the strangely dressed crowd, with their unusual headgear, black eye-coverings, and small boxes continually pressed against their faces. But he braved it. For no sensible reason, he had it in mind that somehow he'd learn more of his mission, though he didn't know how or from whom, if he went to the center of town. He turned right onto the High Street—which had been blocked off to traffic—and weaved his way past the gift shops, take-aways, banks, and news agents. He caught sight of a storefront that had been set up as a tourist display. The tapestries and paintings intrigued him because they were so unlike the color posters and photographs he had seen plastered to every other available space. These were more in the style of art from Arthur's time. He walked into the building to have a look around.

It was a tourist information center, set up to detail the town's history and provide visitors with maps and helpful information. Arthur went to the counter and rifled through the free pamphlets to find a map, in hopes of discerning where he was. Since the map was in English, he used the positions of the three hills to help him remember. To his delight, he found a mark for the Chalice Well, known better to Arthur as the Chalk Well. That would be as good a starting point as any—if only to see what they'd done to the landmarks he cherished the most.

He turned to leave the building but glimpsed a glass-encased display with Latin writing. He went to it with hopes that it might tell him more than the nonsensical literature scattered around the room.

The display contained paintings, photos, and replicas of old manuscripts. The Latin was fragmentary, found only in the manuscripts themselves. It took him a moment to realize that the display was about the life of King Arthur—*his* life. He laughed at the butchered retelling of his battle against invading Romans, particularly when the story claimed that the Romans were giants. He was then surprised to find himself moved by the rather accurate account of how he had banished Lancelot after finding out that Lancelot and Guinevere were adulterers. The vision misted up from his tears. He didn't want to read any more.

But he couldn't pull himself away. For the first time, it occurred to him that from the vantage point of the future, he could find out how he ultimately died. Was it of old age? Maybe he died in his sleep after restoring his kingdom to its former glory. That's what he hoped to learn. His heart trembled as he followed the sequence of pictures to their conclusion. Most of them were in English, but a final matted photo of an ancient manuscript had enough Latin for Arthur to read his own end. It was a mistake, he knew instantly. More than any mortal should know.

Legend says that King Arthur and his wicked nephew Mordred fatally wounded one another in battle, the display read.

He clenched his fists, crumpling the map, as he raced away from the display, out the front door, and onto the pedestrian mall. *Slain by Mordred!* he cried within himself. The words burned through his body like fever in his veins. *Slain by Mordred.* So that was the end of the battle he had been about to fight when this nightmare began.

Arthur pushed his way back down the High Street in the same direction he'd come. At that moment he needed to see and to touch something from his own time. He needed comfort and knew that there was one place in Glastonbury where he'd find it.

Walking anxiously south on Chilkwell Street, Arthur unhappily joined a crowd of tourists who had come to see what he hoped to see: the Chalk Well. He felt claustrophobic as they entered through a manicured garden and followed a path to a small stone wall with a lion's head carved in the center. Water streamed from the lion's mouth.

The well, Arthur thought, relieved. It didn't look the same as it had in his time, but he was grateful that no one had built a large building on it. The water still flowed from some mysterious spring deep beneath the Mendip Hills. Arthur pressed forward to touch the water, to wash his face with it, to drink in its healing powers. He was squeezed out by the other tourists who clamored to get cups and glasses under the spout for a drink. Arthur watched angrily. Their vacant smiles and incessant chatter made his blood boil. Didn't they understand where they were? He wanted to yell at them to kneel, to be reverent. Didn't they realize how sacred this place was? It was here that blood-colored water had poured out to bring healing to the sick and infirm. Joseph of Arimathea himself had brought about the miracle! Didn't they know that this entire area was holy ground and should be dealt with respectfully? His fists still clenched, Arthur raised them to strike out at the infidels. He wanted violently to teach them respect and honor. He wanted to thrust them all aside so he could treat the well with the reverence it was worthy to receive.

At that moment, the threatening clouds above suddenly yielded their rain in large, heavy drops that opened into a deluge. The tourists scattered for shelter. Thankfully Arthur watched them go and used the intervening seconds to calm himself down. "Legend" said he was slain by Mordred. But legend wasn't always right. Perhaps there was another end the legends didn't know about. Perhaps Arthur thwarted Mordred. Perhaps Arthur could *still* thwart Mordred somehow.

The tourists gone, Arthur knelt at the well to confide in his God. The rain poured down his bent head, and his clothes were quickly soaked through. Muddied rivulets mixed with tears and ran into his sleeves from his clasped hands. Oblivious, he prayed.

The rain continued to fall as Arthur emerged from the garden and followed Chilkwell Street up to a large parklike area. He crossed the road, dodging cars as he did, and entered the park from the east. He kept his gaze fixed on the place where the church of Joseph of Arimathea had once stood. It was gone. Now there stood several tall ruins of churches Arthur didn't recognize. Again, it gave him a tight-chested feeling. Again, he was a man out of place and time. How many churches had been built and destroyed? What truly had become of the people Arthur knew and loved the most? They were buried deep in places of fallen stone and thick moss.

Where had *he* been buried after being toppled by a thrust of Mordred's sword?

Arthur sat down on the cold and wet stone steps under the arch of one of the ruins. He wished this dream would end. He wished he could return to his own time. Knowing now that his battle with Mordred would be fatal, he could return to alter the events: change the day of the battle, make peace with Mordred, or perhaps have Mordred assassinated in his sleep. But he was helpless to do anything at all until he could go back to his time. *God, why am I here?* he asked as he put his face in his hands. He was a forlorn figure in the gray rain.

A hand fell lightly onto his shoulder. He lifted his head slowly and looked up into the face of Merlin.

CHAPTER 28

"It's you, isn't it?" Myrddin asked with misty eyes.

"God save us," Arthur gasped in Latin.

Myrddin grinned, barely able to keep from dancing among the ruins. "You *do* speak Latin. Of course you would. What other language would you know? Ancient Celtic perhaps? Latin. I should have thought of it myself."

Arthur leapt to his feet and embraced Myrddin in a bone-crunching hug. "I prayed to God for help. He has answered my prayers. You are here, old friend."

Graham, who'd been standing several feet away like a reluctant witness, took a few steps forward. He was afraid the hug might turn into something more violent.

"Is this your traveler from the church?" Myrddin asked Graham after Arthur returned him to his own two feet.

"One and the same," Graham nodded. "What's this all about?"

Myrddin patted Arthur on the arm and spoke slowly in Latin. "Sire, I would like you to meet the Reverend Graham Peters of Christ Church in Wellsbridge."

Arthur bowed. "I was lost, and this good priest gave me aid this morning. I am grateful to you."

"Nice to meet you," Graham said quickly, then turned to Myrddin. "Myrddin? What's going on here?"

"Graham," Myrddin began, but stopped. The words caught in his throat as tears of happiness spilled from his eyes. He quickly brushed them aside. "Forgive me. I'm . . . proud to introduce you to . . . King Arthur."

Graham tilted his head forward and rubbed his eyes wearily. "Oh, God, have mercy on the feebleminded."

"What?" Myrddin exclaimed. "You still don't believe?"

Graham sucked in his breath as if it were the only way to control his anger. "I'm going back to Wellsbridge. I only hope I can catch a cab." He turned and walked away.

"What will it take to make you believe?" Myrddin called after him. His voice bounced with the rainfall around the ruins.

A tall, thin man with an open umbrella stepped out from under an archway. "Maybe I can help," he said.

Graham looked around to see who had spoken.

A young boy, probably in his mid-teens, appeared next to the man. He looked wet and slightly bewildered.

Myrddin scrutinized the intruders, unsure of their place in this scene.

"My name is Malcolm Dubbs," the man said simply. "I think we all have a lot to talk about."

Arthur raised his face to the rain and laughed.

The five of them gathered in a room at an inn Malcolm had found between Glastonbury and Wellsbridge. The rain lashed at the window as they drank hot coffee, tea and, for Arthur, a large ale. Malcolm explained to an enthusiastic Myrddin and a skeptical Graham everything that had happened and the various theories they'd had along the way about *why* it was happening. Myrddin translated the account to Arthur who, considering his despondency at the abbey ruin, seemed happy in a childlike way.

"It's obvious that he was displaced in time," Malcolm said in conclusion, "though we haven't been able to figure out exactly why. We guessed only that he belonged here in England, so we brought him here. The rest is still a mystery."

Graham remembered meeting Malcolm when he'd come to secure the church ruin. That had seemed indulgent. This was insane. "You seem like mature, reasonable men—for Americans. I can't believe I'm sitting here listening to this. You honestly think that this man is Arthur, and he's come shooting through time for . . . for some purpose?"

Malcolm nodded.

"Why?" Graham challenged. "Why is he here?"

"Because I called him," Myrddin said.

All eyes turned to the old man as he translated for Arthur.

"I called you," he repeated. "I blew the horn that called you from the Cave of Dreams."

"Where have you been all these years, dear friend? You disappeared and left me alone," Arthur replied.

"Sire, we must keep our minds fixed on the task at hand."

"You have returned to aid me in my fight against Mordred," Arthur said hopefully.

"Myrddin," Graham reminded him, "you have a non-Latin-speaking public to consider."

Myrddin gazed at Arthur, then addressed his audience. "I said that I blew the horn that called the king from the Cave of Dreams," Myrddin said.

"The Cave of Dreams?" Malcolm asked. "What is that?"

Myrddin shrugged. "It is where the reality of the past resides in the dreams of the present."

"What's that mean?" Jeff queried.

Myrddin shrugged again. "I suppose in your terminology, you'd call it a crack in time or a fault line. I never questioned *how* King Arthur would return. I simply knew in faith that he would. God often sends us help in the most peculiar ways."

"And in the most peculiar places. Arthur wound up in America rather than here," Malcolm observed.

"Part of the mystery." Myrddin smiled whimsically.

Jeff raised his hand as if he were in school. "Wait a minute. Help? Who needs his help?"

Myrddin said, "Britain needs Arthur now more than ever."

"Why now?" Graham had a look on his face that said he was playing along, but not believing any of it.

"You more than anyone should know the answer to that question," Myrddin said with a hint of rebuke.

"I have felt it since arriving in this dream," Arthur said boldly. He hit his fist against the small table next to his chair. The tea cups rattled. "There is a battle to be fought!"

Myrddin leaned toward Arthur, his finger poised like a teacher's pointer. "This isn't a battle of strength, sire, but of character and honor. It's a spiritual battle, of sorts. Are you prepared to fight that kind of battle?"

Arthur looked as if he might speak, then sat back in a thoughtful silence.

"But what *kind* of battle?" Graham, who had grasped most of their exchange, asked impatiently. "And don't tell me I should know better than anyone else, because I *don't* know."

"That," Myrddin said, "is what we'll learn as we go along."

Graham rubbed his forehead as if he had a headache. "As we go along to where? Do you have any idea how ridiculous this sounds?"

Myrddin nodded. "I do. I've spent most of my life being called ridiculous."

"That's not what I mean," Graham said as he stood up. "I don't have time for this little game. I have a church to save."

Malcolm pushed the curtain aside. The rain stopped. "Reverend Peters—"

"Graham."

"Graham, would you mind if we went to see your church?" Malcolm asked.

"I don't mind at all. Why?"

"Because it might help us all if we saw it. Particularly now that we know that it's where this whole adventure began."

In his room, Adrian was stretched out on his bed with his arms tucked behind his head. He'd been staring at the ceiling for more than an hour. He didn't know what else to do while the war of his feelings raged inside his head and heart. He was angry at himself, angry with Ponsonby, guilt stricken, and embarrassed.

Did I imagine our deal, or did Ponsonby dupe me? he wondered. *Was I played for a fool?*

But did the answer really matter? Deal or dupe, friend or fool, either way his father had been betrayed at Adrian's hand. He had played Judas well, except he didn't do it for thirty pieces of silver. He had done it for . . . for what? What was he really thinking when he blabbed to Ponsonby what he knew about the church's condition? If not thirty pieces of silver, what was he after? Security? Peace of mind? A hope for his future? A way to get back at his father's weakness?

Probably all of the above, he thought sourly. Ponsonby was everything his father wasn't: strong, determined, successful. He was charming and beguiling. He had taught Adrian the ways of the world—at least, of his world—a world of money and cars and dreams that you could actually wrap your hands around and put in your pocket. It was a world where you could be the bully rather than bullied. It was a world where you were the master of the game rather than just a pawn moved about by those more cunning and powerful than you. That was Ponsonby's world, and it was awfully attractive. After a lifetime of watching his father play servant, washing other men's feet, it was refreshing to believe in an alternative. But . . . was that really what Adrian believed?

What do you believe in? Whom do you believe in? Those were the questions Ponsonby demanded that Adrian answer.

He suddenly sat up and swung his legs off of the bed. His foot kicked what was left of the daily paper on the floor. Adrian looked down and nudged it with his toe. As it moved, his eye caught a glimpse of the small paragraph about King Arthur's arrival in England. He and Lewis had laughed when they read it earlier on their way back from York.

But for just a moment he wished it were true. He wished he could believe in things like that again. For if he could believe in a world where the unexplainable happened, then maybe he could believe in his father's world rather than Ponsonby's. What kind of meaning did money have in a world of miracles?

What do you believe in?

He stood up and walked to the window, where he yanked the curtain aside and looked out into the fading day. The rain clouds from that afternoon had moved on to other places, allowing the sun just a couple of hours before it was time to go down.

What's it going to be? he asked, willing himself to make up his mind. Did he believe in his father's way or Ponsonby's? Was he set to be a faithful pushover or a cynical nonbeliever?

He thought of his friends in Wellsbridge and the more superficial acquaintances he had made at school. Did they ever make a decision like this? Did they reach this kind of fork in the road—or did they merely ride along, allowing the road to take them wherever it did? Maybe he was alone. Maybe no one else ever had to make the same kind of choice.

One way or another, he had to decide. He couldn't stay in limbo forever. Ponsonby would demand his loyalty further if he planned to stay at the manor. And, if his mother's tone on the phone was an indicator, he couldn't go home unless he was prepared to apologize and commit in some small way to respecting his father.

He had to decide what he believed.

And then he had to *do* something about it.

CHAPTER 30

The five crowded into Malcolm's rental car and drove to Christ Church. Graham was dismayed to see Ponsonby's Land Rover in the lot. *He's like a vulture hovering and waiting*, he thought.

As they unfolded themselves out of the small car, Graham saw Ponsonby and a balding man with glasses emerge from the church.

"Ah! Reverend Peters." Ponsonby smiled toothily. "Glad you're here."

Graham was working on a snappy retort when Arthur, who had just climbed out of the car, suddenly roared and charged at Ponsonby. A confused cry went up from the four men, who instantly chased after him.

"Good heavens!" Ponsonby exclaimed and ducked behind his companion, who looked stricken. Arthur grabbed Ponsonby's companion with one hand and tossed him aside like a rag doll. He then lunged at Ponsonby, who had the good sense and quick skill to jump in the other direction. Arthur narrowly missed him.

"What's this all about?" Ponsonby shouted.

By this time Graham, Malcolm, and Jeff had formed a tentative wall between Arthur and Ponsonby while Myrddin grabbed Arthur. "What are you doing, sire? Why are you attacking this man?"

"Do you not know him? Has he bewitched you? It is Mordred!"

"No, sire, no," Myrddin said. "You are mistaken."

"He has followed me into this dream! He has come to slay me!" Arthur said. Then he shouted at Ponsonby, "I know your wicked ways, vile betrayer! Stand and fight!"

"Sire, please," Myrddin pleaded. With great effort, he guided Arthur around the corner of the church. Their voices, arguing in Latin, could be heard after they were out of sight.

"What on earth is the matter with the man?" Ponsonby scowled.

Jeff helped the balding man to his feet. "Are you all right, sir?"

"The name's Clydesdale and, no, I am not all right. Lunatics like that should be put away." Clydesdale dusted himself off.

"Sorry." Jeff gave him his glasses, which had been knocked off.

"Is this your way of dealing with your problems?" Ponsonby asked Graham. "Bring in a team of ruffians?"

"Obviously, he thought you were someone else," Graham replied. "What brings you to a *closed* church at this time of day?"

"Clydesdale and I were looking over the grounds for . . . future planning."

Graham folded his arms. "Aren't you slightly premature?"

"Am I?"

"I've been given three days to come up with the money for renovations," Graham said.

Ponsonby laughed. "You don't really believe you can accomplish that kind of fund-raising in such a short amount of time."

Graham smiled. "Stranger things have happened."

Ponsonby ignored him and turned to Malcolm and Jeff, who introduced themselves.

"Malcolm Dubbs bought the oldest section of the church," Graham said dryly. "Would you like to send some inspectors over to have it condemned?"

Ponsonby grinned without amusement. "I'm sure America has inspectors of its own." He signaled abruptly to Clydesdale, and they walked toward the Land Rover. "It's been interesting meeting you. And I suggest you put the tall hairy one on a leash."

Inside the Land Rover, Clydesdale said, "Outrageous behavior. Do you think Peters did all that on purpose?"

Preoccupied, Ponsonby started the motor. "No, he's not that clever, or stupid."

"Then what's their game?"

"I have no idea," Ponsonby said. He put the car into gear and pulled away from the church. "Clydesdale, do you understand Latin?"

"No."

Ponsonby grunted. "I do."

Graham, Malcolm, and Jeff walked around the church in the

same direction Myrddin and Arthur had gone.

"They must be where your ruin used to sit," Graham said. His voice was tense. Malcolm wondered if it was because of the confrontation with Ponsonby or because he resented Malcolm having part of the church in America.

They found Arthur wearing a defiant expression and sitting on a large stone as Myrddin paced in front of him. They cut off their heated discussion as soon as the others joined them.

"Problems?" Graham asked wryly.

Myrddin threw his hands up. "He's being unreasonable."

"It's nice to know we weren't the only ones who couldn't control him," Jeff chuckled.

"He has it all wrong," Myrddin went on. "He thinks he's here to defeat Ponsonby."

Graham smiled. "He gets my vote for that."

"He thinks Ponsonby is Mordred," Myrddin explained irritably.

"If you're going to pretend that he's King Arthur, then why not pretend that Ponsonby is Mordred? Let them have it out to the bitter end," Graham said scornfully.

Myrddin frowned at Graham.

"Gentlemen," Graham said, bowing politely, "this is where I say good night. I don't know what you're going to do now, but I hope your Arthurian romance ends the way you want it to. Maybe you'll have some swashbuckling derring-do or save a damsel in distress. Better still, the prime minister might invite you round for tea to hear about Arthur's great mission. I look forward to reading all about it in the tabloids." He ambled off toward his house.

"He isn't normally like this. It's this church business," Myrddin told them.

"I don't blame him," Malcolm offered. "Everything that's happened is pretty far-fetched. And he brought up a valid point."

"What's that?" Jeff asked.

"What *are* we supposed to do now?"

CHAPTER 31

The four remaining men returned to Malcolm's room at the inn. Malcolm wanted to go to a restaurant for dinner, then he remembered Arthur's eating habits and thought better of it. He had food delivered to the room. After they'd eaten, Jeff knelt in front of the small television set on a table in the corner. Malcolm, Myrddin, and Arthur pulled out various maps and spread them on the bed. Malcolm was sure that part of the mystery about Arthur and his mission was connected to where he was before he came to the present.

"I believe his mission will reveal itself to us," Myrddin proclaimed. "We don't have to search for it."

"Maybe you're right," Malcolm said. "Or maybe we have a part to play in how it's revealed. Please ask Arthur to show us what he can on the maps."

Myrddin was skeptical, but translated anyway. "Can you look at this map and tell us where you were when you fell asleep?"

Arthur pointed at an area called Salisbury Plain. "We gathered our armies here." He rifled through several of Malcolm's maps until he found one of the Glastonbury area. "Where are we now?"

Myrddin pointed to the area where the inn was situated.

"The church?"

Myrddin ran his finger along the paper and stopped at the small symbol of the cross indicating the church.

Malcolm tugged at his ear. "Why would he fall asleep in his tent on Salisbury Plain, but wind up in a church ruin in Fawlt Line? Granted, you summoned him with the horn—"

"Yes, I've been doing that faithfully for years."

"You mean you've been going up to the tower and blowing the horn every night?" Jeff asked in wonder.

"Not every night. Near holy days, mostly."

"But why?"

"Because I believed he would come."

146

"Yes, he came," Malcolm said, not wanting to lose track of their conversation. "But he came to the church ruin in America. Why?"

"I thought you already established the connection between the church ruin in Fawlt Line and the church in Wellsbridge," Myrddin said.

Arthur pointed to the map again. "What does this symbol mean?"

"It's a symbol for a manor house, sire."

"Manor house?"

"Yes. In this case, it belongs to Mr. Ponsonby," Myrddin told him.

Arthur nodded thoughtfully and put the map away.

Malcolm continued, "We established the connection between my church ruin and Christ Church, that's true. Maybe Arthur showed up there because that's where the ruin was. Which means that he was supposed to show up here in Wellsbridge."

"A worthy consideration," Myrddin nodded.

"But why the church at Wellsbridge? Why not wake up at the Abbey ruin in Glastonbury or Cadbury or any of the sites more generally acknowledged as places connected with Arthur?" Malcolm asked.

Myrddin's face lit up. "Perhaps Arthur wasn't buried in Glastonbury after all, as the legends said. Perhaps his body *was* carried away by the Lady of the Lake to another place nearby—to Wellsbridge, which also would have been an island at the time. Perhaps everyone has had it all wrong by a couple of miles."

"That's exactly what I was thinking."

"Do you really believe a lady in a lake carried him away in a boat?" Jeff asked from his place in front of the television.

"Do you really believe that King Arthur is standing here in front of you right now?" Malcolm retorted.

Jeff got the point and returned to flipping channels.

Arthur announced that he was tired and wanted to sleep. Malcolm showed him the connecting room and began to explain where everything was, but Arthur seemed impatient to be left alone. Malcolm obliged him.

Myrddin was beside himself when Malcolm returned. "I must phone Graham and tell him!"

"Tell him what?"

"This bit of information about his church!"

Malcolm didn't get it. "What about it?"

"It may be the miracle he's been looking for. Establishing a connection between Christ Church and King Arthur could save it as an historical landmark!"

"Who will believe it?" Graham asked in a sour voice from the other end of the line. Since the rooms weren't equipped with telephones, Myrddin had phoned Graham from a pay phone in the lobby of the inn.

"Why wouldn't they?" Myrddin asked.

Graham chuckled, "Oh, I see. They're going to take your word for it? Or maybe the Americans'? Those are credible sources for British history. Or perhaps you could set up an interview with Arthur, and he'll tell everyone how the Lady of the Lake took him to my church after he died?"

"Graham—"

"No. We're still stuck, Myrddin. Thank you for trying."

Myrddin was disheartened to hear such bitterness in Graham's voice. "You haven't done very well trying to find supporters, I assume."

"In the short time since I left you? Nary a one," Graham said. "Even Anne won't donate. I'm on my own."

"Don't let this defeat you, Graham," Myrddin said. "Good will come from this, I know it. Somehow it all fits together—in a way only God knows."

"Thanks for phoning, Myrddin," Graham replied as if he hadn't heard a word the old sage said.

"Goodnight."

They hung up.

Myrddin walked back to the room. Arthur's return was important for the entire nation, there was no doubt about that, and yet somehow his return seemed more directly related to the events surrounding Christ Church and Graham Peters. It was all connected somehow, but even Myrddin couldn't see how.

Good will come from this, he had said, and he believed it wholeheartedly.

Perhaps the mission was to get Graham to believe it.

"Why do you have only four channels in this country?" Jeff asked as he kept switching the television knob. "It's pretty boring."

"Where is your Uncle Malcolm?"

"In the bathroom brushing his teeth."

"Of course," Myrddin said, suddenly realizing how late it was. "I suppose I should go home now. We can pray for God's guidance in the morning."

He turned to go, then decided to peek in on Arthur. Without knocking, he slowly opened the connecting door, hoping it wouldn't creak on its hinges. The other room was dark and silent. Myrddin assumed Arthur was asleep and started to close the door again. A breeze swept through the room, and Myrddin realized the window must've been left open.

Malcolm stepped out of the bathroom, wiping his face with a towel.

"Did you open Arthur's window?" Myrddin asked him.

"No, I was afraid it might be too cool tonight. Why?"

"Arthur opened it then," Myrddin replied. But an alarm went off in his mind.

With Malcolm behind him, Myrddin pushed into the dark room and fumbled for a light switch. A light on an end table came on. Curtains billowed gently next to the open window. The bed was empty.

CHAPTER 32

Restless and unable to sleep, Graham took a walk through the field between his house and Christ Church. It soothed and calmed him to hear the swish of his feet as they brushed the damp grass. The occasional hoot of an owl or childlike cry of vixens in the nearby woods reminded him that an entirely different world existed and went about its business, untouched by his troubled world. Under a vast starlit sky, Graham's rebellious son, his condemned church, and his potential unemployment seemed minuscule.

With all his worrying and struggling, had he been able to change one iota of what had happened? No. Adrian still went to work for Ponsonby, being influenced in ways Graham hardly dared to think about. Christ Church was still put on the chopping block. Graham's career as a minister in the Church of England was as good as dead.

He looked up at the blinking stars. Was Somebody up there who actually cared about Graham's life? Was this God at work even in the mess that had come up in the past day?

In the deepest part of his heart where a child's faith still endured, Graham hoped so. *His ways are not our ways,* a writer in the Bible had said. How can we possibly hope to understand Him?

We're like actors in a play. It's our task to perform our roles to the best of our abilities even when we don't know what's come before us or what will come after, another writer had said.

Graham had no idea how all the pieces would fall into place. But for just a moment, walking in that field toward the church, he believed that Myrddin might be right. Maybe the pieces would fit together miraculously and everything would turn out all right in the end.

His thoughts became tiny prayers and, in those prayers, Graham felt a flicker of hope. *God,* he said, *I wish you would do something, say something, that might serve as a sign that you really are in the middle of this mess and not asleep somewhere.*

Graham stopped in his tracks and waited. The childlike faith in his heart waited expectantly. The night was still. No sound was made.

Except for the unmistakable sound of stone scraping against stone.

Graham's heart lurched at the sudden thought of a vandal or, more likely, one of Ponsonby's men wreaking further damage on the church. He chased the sound, slowing down when he came to the corner of the church where the ruin had been. He peered around as quietly as he could.

Arthur, if that's who he really was, was busy moving several large stones away from the church wall. That, in and of itself, was unusual enough. What made it more so was that he was dressed in a long cape. Under the cape he wore a tunic with the symbol of a red dragon stitched to the front. His waist was bound by a gold belt, his legs were covered with brown tights, and on his feet were leather shoes.

As Graham watched, Arthur reached into the cavity he'd created by moving the stones. He retrieved something that, for a moment, the size of his body eclipsed from Graham's view. His arms and shoulders went taut from the weight of it. Graham was almost certain he heard a low pulsating hum.

Arthur turned and, in both hands, held a sword in a golden scabbard. It was unlike anything Graham had ever seen. Arthur pulled the sword free from its container, and Graham stifled a gasp of awe. Even in the starlight, it shone like it was lit from the inside-out. Jewels sparkled on the handle. The silver blade danced and dazzled as Arthur tested it against an invisible opponent. It was beautiful. It was majestic. It was . . .

Excalibur, Graham thought. He immediately rebuked himself for thinking it. It couldn't be Excalibur, he reminded himself, because this man wasn't Arthur. He couldn't be—even if he looked exactly as he'd always imagined Arthur would look. It was impossible.

Or was it?

Enough of this tomfoolery, Graham told himself. He meant to step out of the shadows and demand just what in the blue blazes the strange man thought he was doing.

But he didn't. That child in his heart wouldn't let him.

I'll just watch him to make sure he doesn't hurt anyone, Graham rationalized.

Holding the sword by the handle, the stranger pointed it downward at arm's length and plunged it into the ground. He knelt and performed the sign of the cross. Softly, he prayed.

After a moment, he stood up again. He carefully put the sword back into the scabbard and attached it to his belt. Grabbing his bundle of modern clothes, he tossed them into the hole, then strode purposefully across the field and away from the church.

Graham leaned against the cold stone of the building. His practical, gotta-get-up-in-the-morning adult told him to go to bed and forget what he'd just seen. His childlike self told him to go along just to see what kind of adventure might result.

What if he really is King Arthur? the child teased him.

Graham took a deep breath and cautiously slid from the wall to follow.

CHAPTER 33

Adrian made up his mind. He looked out his window into the dark night and tried to muster his courage. His gaze trailed down the darkness to the splash of light on the patio below. It came from Ponsonby's study. Adrian was about to turn toward the door when, out of the corner of his eye, he saw something move. Whatever it was lurked in the shadows near the study windows. It prowled along the wall and entered into the light. Adrian's eyes bulged. It was a man dressed in ancient clothes carrying a gigantic sword.

The figure disappeared into the shadows again.

Adrian stepped back from the window, a wash of mixed emotions on his face. He raced from the room and down a servants' stairway to the door leading outside from the kitchen. He closed the door behind him silently, then hugged the shadows on the wall until he got to the end leading to the patio itself. He slowly peeked around the corner.

In a quick one-two action, a hand grabbed his shirt and another was plastered across his mouth. "Sssshhhh," a voice hissed.

Adrian looked into the eyes of his father. "MMMmmmmphhh!"

"Be quiet, will you?" Graham whispered into his ear.

"What are you doing here? Are you trying to get arrested?"

"I think I'm sleepwalking," Graham answered.

"What's going on? You aren't—" Adrian stopped himself and leaned away to see if his father had lost his mind and dressed up like King Arthur. He passed his eyes over his father's sweatshirt, jeans, and sneakers, and gave a sigh of relief.

"Do you know that Ponsonby has never invited me over?" Graham said glibly. "It's looks like a nice manor in the dark."

"Dad, why are you here?"

"Why are *you* here?" Graham retorted. "Are you simply strolling the grounds or, as Ponsonby's lackey, do you come out to protect him from prowlers carrying large swords?"

Adrian's eyes went wide again. "I didn't imagine it!"

"Oh, he's real," Graham said. "But I have no idea what he's up to. Imagine my surprise when I followed him here."

"Where did he go?" Adrian asked.

"I don't know. I followed too far behind. But I suspect I should go home like a good little boy and, like a *bad* little boy, you should go back inside to your master."

"Dad, please. There's something we need to talk about."

"You *are* talking to me, then?" Graham said.

"Will you stop being so sarcastic? You sound like . . . like me," Adrian complained.

Graham agreed. "We'll talk after we find our Superhero. We can't let him run loose around the grounds."

They started off, but Adrian stopped again. "Dad, is he really King Arthur?"

"I haven't the foggiest idea," Graham replied. "To be honest, I hope he is."

"Me too."

"Now which way do you suggest we go?"

Adrian looked around. "To the other side of the patio. That's the direction he was headed when I saw him from my window."

They crept across the patio fearfully. Adrian heard voices from an open window and stopped. Beyond the thin white curtains, he saw two men walk into the room. "Hang on. It's Ponsonby and his pal Clydesdale. What could they be up to at this time of night?"

"Don't you know?" Graham asked sarcastically. "I thought you were in Ponsonby's fullest confidence."

Adrian ignored the comment and moved to the window, keeping to the edge of the shadows. Graham followed him. Ponsonby was typing on his computer keyboard. "All in all a good day's work," he said.

"As soon as you transfer the money into the proper accounts, we'll get the rest of it sorted out," Clydesdale said. "They're anxious to put it to an end, particularly the councilmen."

"I have it all here," Ponsonby told him as he tapped his computer screen. "Tell them to relax. Peters can't do a thing. He's a wet fish who wouldn't know how to start a fight, let alone win one."

"I resent that," Graham whispered in protest.

"Well, it's true," Adrian said.

Graham growled, "Oh, and I suppose you think that fighting the way Ponsonby fights is the way to win?"

"Ssshhh," Adrian hissed, his attention on the two men inside.

"It's done," Ponsonby said.

Clydesdale smiled and adjusted his glasses. "In that case, I'll go home. I want to be at their offices bright and early tomorrow."

"You do that." Ponsonby grinned and walked with him to the hall. "Rest assured you'll have a bonus on the other end of this."

The two men disappeared into the hall, and Adrian guessed Ponsonby was walking Clydesdale to the front door. "Quick, give me a leg up," Adrian said.

"What?"

"I want to have a look at that screen." Adrian began scaling the wall to the window even without his father's help.

"You live here, remember?" Graham said.

Adrian hooked his arms on the sill and pulled himself into the study. "He never lets me near his computer unless he's there. I think he's paying people off, Dad."

Against his better judgment, Graham gave Adrian a hard push through the window. Adrian hit the floor with a thump.

Graham watched anxiously from the patio as Adrian scrolled up and down the screen, then quickly punched some keys on the keyboard. There were voices in the hall. Graham's heart jumped to his throat. "Come out of there, son," Graham whispered harshly.

"Just a minute. I almost have it," Adrian whispered in reply. "Go around to the front door and stall him. Tell him you want to talk about the church—anything—"

Graham's best sensibilities told him he shouldn't be in this position. Who did he think he was, Humphrey Bogart? Normal people didn't do things like this. But for the sake of his son, he rushed into the darkness, heading for the front of the house.

He had just disappeared when Ponsonby returned to his study.

CHAPTER 34

"He was here," Myrddin said after investigating the side of Christ Church where the ruins had been. Malcolm and Jeff were with him.

"What makes you so sure?"

Myrddin pulled Arthur's "modern clothes" from the hole he'd made in the stones.

"I hope he's not running around naked somewhere," Malcolm said.

"No, I'm sure he's dressed." Myrddin scouted around the area. The headlights of Malcolm's car made the old man's bony shadow bounce on the church wall.

Malcolm was puzzled. "Why did he come here?"

"To get his clothes," Jeff answered. "And Excalibur!"

"Of course!" Malcolm said. "This is where they went from the church ruin in Fawlt Line. I should have known. I thought he was acting suspiciously when we were here earlier."

Myrddin stalked around nervously. "If he has Excalibur, then I know where he's gone. Ponsonby's."

"Why there?"

"Arthur thinks that Ponsonby is Mordred."

"But it's obvious that he's not."

"It doesn't matter," Myrddin explained. "You have to see things the way Arthur sees them. The people of his day were steeped in the power of symbols, not logic. Forces were at work then that we don't understand, and often they were captured in symbols. The Cross of Christ symbolized sacrifice, goodness, redemption. Excalibur symbolized power and authority. The Grail symbolized God's blessing on Britain. Even the king himself symbolized purity of heart and virtue. Mordred symbolized corruption, ruthless ambition, and evil."

"But that was Mordred a long time ago," Jeff stated. "What does Arthur think he can do to Ponsonby now?"

"He said today that if Britain is in a spiritual crisis, then Mordred and his kind are the cause. From his experience, there's only one way to deal with such men."

"How?" Jeff asked.

"Kill them," Myrddin replied.

"Let's go," Malcolm said.

CHAPTER 35

"What do you think you're doing?" Ponsonby demanded.

Adrian stood frozen in front of the computer.

Ponsonby scowled. "What a waste of skin you are. I was prepared to train you, to be your mentor. This is how you repay me?"

He closed the double doors to the study, then slowly crossed the room. "Do you have any idea how many young men would like to sit at my feet just to learn what I know? You had the chance. But you've blown it, Adrian. I asked you to make a choice. Like your father, you've made the wrong one."

"Have I?" Adrian said in a thin voice.

"You're trembling like him, too," Ponsonby said with a laugh.

"Maybe that's because I *am* like him," Adrian said defiantly. "There was never a choice for me. I'll take his love and his faith over your cruel and heartless car collection any day!"

Somehow it didn't come out as grand as he'd hoped, but the meaning was clear.

Ponsonby was at the edge of the desk now. "You have your father's way with words, too." He grabbed Adrian by the arm, dragged him to a large chair near the desk, and pushed him into it.

"What are you going to do? You can't keep me here. You can't do anything to me," Adrian said, wanting to believe it.

"Well, now, let's consider our options," Ponsonby said. "I suppose I could have you arrested for breaking and entering, stealing valuable goods." He raised his finger as if he'd thought of a good idea. "That one has potential. You could be knocked unconscious in the antiques display room, as if I'd caught you there trying to steal my Ming vase."

The thought of being knocked unconscious by Ponsonby in any room didn't appeal to Adrian. *Where are you, Dad?*

Ponsonby smiled. "Come to think of it, the scandal of Reverend Peters' son being arrested for theft will make my job a lot easier. Thank you, Adrian. You have your father's knack for being useful in all the wrong ways."

The doorbell rang, followed by relentless pounding.

Ponsonby turned to his desk and hit the talk button on the small intercom there. "Leave it! No one answer that door!" he shouted to the staff. "It's an intruder! Call the police!"

Ponsonby chuckled as he turned to face Adrian again. He was startled to find the boy out of the chair. He was even more startled when Adrian socked him in the jaw.

Ponsonby responded by slugging Adrian in the stomach. "You're a pest, do you know that?"

Adrian fell to the floor.

Not satisfied, Ponsonby grabbed Adrian and yanked him roughly to his feet. He drew his arm back to throw another punch when the windows suddenly exploded, as if a wrecking ball had come through the glass.

Ponsonby and Adrian stumbled backward, shielding themselves from the flying shards.

Just outside, King Arthur hacked away at the panes, sills, and frames with his sword. Having cleared a way, he hoisted himself in one swift move into the study.

"You again!" Ponsonby cried, more annoyed than frightened.

"Look well to yourself," Arthur said in Latin, while Excalibur waved menacingly in front of him. "I will have you this night and will thwart your evil doings on this land and the evil you would do to me in battle tomorrow."

"You're a lunatic!" Ponsonby shouted back. "Who do you think you are in that ridiculous costume? In what novelty shop did you buy that sword?"

"You are a villain and traitor both," Arthur said. "Prepare to die."

"I was a master swordsman at Cambridge. I have no intention of dying," Ponsonby said. He swung around toward the fireplace and grabbed one of the crossed swords hanging above it. Without a word of warning, he brought it around with a crash against Excalibur.

CHAPTER 36

Adrian saw his chance and scrambled to safety behind the chair. With wide-eyed fascination he watched the two men fight. Arthur and Ponsonby rained powerful blows on each other and thrust and parried with remarkable skill. Adrian felt that he'd been transported to another time to witness a fierce battle between two old enemies. The men's grunts and loud *chings!* of steel on steel brought some of the servants to the study door. But Ponsonby had locked it, and all they could do was stand outside and pound loudly until someone found a key. The clamor seemed to add to the intensity of the fight as the two men sped up their attacks and defenses. They crashed into the furniture and slashed the decorations on every flat surface, including the walls.

Graham appeared at the window with a handful of the servants. "Adrian! Son! Are you all right?"

Adrian signaled he was, then shouted, "Stay back! Don't try to come in or you'll get hurt."

Arthur, who didn't have the benefit of being a master swordsman at any university, was the stronger and more skillful fighter. He drove Ponsonby into the corner of the room and hit his sword relentlessly with one blow after another. Ponsonby went down on his knees and cried out in Latin for Arthur to have mercy. With a flick of Excalibur, Arthur knocked Ponsonby's sword out of his hands, then aimed the tip at Ponsonby's neck.

"Have mercy on me," Ponsonby pleaded again in Latin. His face was pallid and drenched in sweat. "I'll do whatever you ask."

The double doors of the study were finally pulled open by a wary butler. Myrddin pushed his way through with Malcolm and Jeff behind him.

"Arthur!" Myrddin shouted.

Arthur respectfully turned to him.

"This is not the way! It wasn't in your time, nor in ours," he appealed. "Ponsonby and his kind will only be defeated by the faithful—men and women of true character whose hopes are set on the things beyond this life."

Arthur looked from Myrddin to Ponsonby and back at Myrddin again.

"In all your years as king, did you ever find that the sword brought anything but pain and misery?"

Arthur didn't answer.

Myrddin went on, "This isn't why you are here, sire. Not for murder."

Arthur leveled his gaze on Ponsonby and tapped his chin with the flat of his blade. "Confess your treachery against God and man," Arthur demanded.

"I confess."

"Give half of your lands and wealth to the poor," Arthur added.

Ponsonby paused and lowered his head.

"Speak, traitor."

"I agree," Ponsonby said.

"Restore the church."

Ponsonby nodded. "Done."

Arthur stepped away and replaced Excalibur in its scabbard. No sooner had he done this than there was another commotion at the door, and three policemen arrived. One immediately rushed to Ponsonby. "You all right, Mr. Ponsonby?"

Ponsonby stood up. "Of course I'm not all right. Do I look all right? Does this room look all right? I want you to arrest that madman for breaking and entering, destroying private property, assault and battery. . . . And watch him, he's dangerous."

The three constables turned to Arthur, who knew in any language that Ponsonby had gone back on his word.

"Throw the sword to the floor, sir," one of the constables said.

Ponsonby laughed. "He only speaks Latin. This is classic. Absolutely classic."

"What has the liar done? What do they want?" Arthur asked Myrddin.

Myrddin glared at Ponsonby, then frowned at Arthur. "They want to take you to prison."

"Brilliant," Ponsonby laughed derisively. "King Arthur in prison. I'll have to get pictures."

The constables closed in on Arthur, who quickly glanced around, checking his options. Suddenly he pushed the policemen aside and, in a few giant steps, left the way he'd come in.

The police shouted and gave chase, scrambling as best as they could through the remnants of the shattered window.

Ponsonby wiped his brow, then turned to Adrian to take care of unfinished business.

But Adrian was gone. So were Myrddin, Malcolm, Jeff and Graham.

Ponsonby picked up the phone.

CHAPTER 37

" 'Give me a leg up,' you said. And I did! What was I thinking? None of this would've happened if I'd dragged you home right then and there." Graham's voice echoed off of the walls and stained-glass windows of Christ Church as he marched back and forth in front of the first pew where Adrian was seated.

Malcolm, Jeff, and Myrddin sat mutely in pews nearby. Introductions had been sorted out on the way, but now there seemed little to be said. Arthur sat dejectedly next to the stone altar, his head lowered into his arms. They were a bedraggled crew. Somewhere a door creaked on its hinges.

"Don't be so certain," Myrddin corrected him. "These events may have been set into motion regardless."

"Here we go again," Graham groaned.

"I had to see what was on the computer," Adrian said. "It was my only chance to . . . to undo the damage I've done."

"Which damage in particular?" Graham asked.

Adrian hesitated, then decided to throw all of his cards on the table. "I was the one who told him about the foundation." He hung his head. He hadn't expected this scene to be played out in front of strangers. He braced himself for his father's anger.

Graham looked toward the back of the church, then knelt next to the pew and faced Adrian directly. His tone was soft. "Why, son?"

" I thought . . . it would free you," Adrian said. "I thought if you lost this church and the archdeacon sent us somewhere else you'd—we'd—be happier. I was sick of people like Ponsonby and the archdeacon bullying you around. I got it all wrong. I'm sorry."

"Did you hear that, Anne?" Graham suddenly called out.

Everyone looked around, confused. Anne, who had caused the door to creak the moment before, walked down the aisle.

"I heard," she said as she arrived at the front pew.

Adrian looked helplessly at his parents.

Graham gazed at his son silently for a moment. "Son, we knew all along that you had told Ponsonby."

"You did?"

"It wasn't hard to figure out."

"Why didn't you say something?" Adrian asked.

"What could we say? We all make our choices."

Adrian put his face in his hands. "I feel awful. I made my choice, but I wanted to take it back. That's why I went into the office. I thought I could fix it before you found out."

Anne lightly stroked the back of his neck. "It's all right, Adrian. We all make bad choices sometimes."

Graham leaned close to Adrian's covered face. "Son, I had no idea how you felt—about me, my job, being here in Wellsbridge. So I'm sorry too. For all of it."

Adrian lifted his head. The three of them looked at each other, and volumes of unspoken words passed between them.

Graham chuckled. "Well, Myrddin, you said there would be a miracle when Arthur came, and there has been."

"Let's hope this atmosphere of forgiveness goes on after they arrest us all," Myrddin said wryly.

"Arrest us!" Jeff exclaimed.

"You don't think Ponsonby is going to just forget about it and go to sleep, do you? He'll make good on his charges against Adrian and most assuredly Arthur," Myrddin said.

Arthur entreated Myrddin to translate what was being said. After Myrddin did, Arthur suddenly slapped his hand against the marble floor that made up part of the altar area. "What now, Merlin? I was a failure before this dream began, and I am a failure now."

"Sire, it's not true." He turned to the rest and said in English, "He thinks it's his fault. He failed."

"If I could figure out what in the world was going on, I'd say we all failed," Malcolm observed.

"Is this some sort of therapy group?" Anne asked.

Arthur continued with a deep sadness in his voice, "In the past and in the present, I chose wrongly. The glory of Camelot was always overshadowed by my failures."

Myrddin sat down next to Arthur. "You're right, of course."

Arthur looked at him, surprised.

"It's the folly of almost every king," Myrddin went on. "You failed only when you pursued your own glory, with a prideful heart, instead of the glory of God."

"You speak truth, old sage. Only now after all these years can I bear to hear it," he said mournfully.

"Perhaps that's why you're here, sire—to learn this lesson before your battle against Mordred—so that when you face him, you face him not with your glory in mind, but God's glory," Myrddin suggested.

"It is my final battle, if your stories are correct," Arthur reminded him.

Myrddin smiled wearily. "Is it ever too late to learn a lesson as important as that? Down to our last battle, our last minute, our last breath, it is worth remembering. The glory of Camelot fades just as all manmade glory fades, but the glory of God transcends this life and goes on forever."

Arthur unhooked Excalibur from his belt and laid it next to Myrddin. "Your wisdom is great, as always. I must face the evil of Mordred on the battlefield in my own time—not here in this dream. Not by the power of the sword, but by God's power alone. God's will be done."

Myrddin switched from Latin to English as he stood up, a wizened preacher now in his pulpit. "It's a lesson for all of us. We've been striving so hard to save this church: playing power games as if they mattered at all. The future of this physical church shouldn't be our primary concern—it's a glory that fades. The spiritual future of our nation is far more important and will never fade so long as it burns bright in the hearts of true believers. What do you believe, Graham?" he suddenly asked. "Do you believe that you are called by God to preach, to be a minister in His church? Can Ponsonby or the archdeacon stop you from that calling? No. They may stop your career, but since when is God's calling in your life supposed to be a career? If you believe in God's calling, then you can't be stopped. *What do you believe?* Do you believe in miracles?"

"I'm starting to . . . again."

"Do you believe that this man is King Arthur?"

Graham blushed. "I'm willing to concede that, yes, he might be King Arthur. Though it's beyond me why I would think so."

"Might be! Beyond you!" Myrddin cried, his face shining and his voice practically rattling the windows. "What is it you want, Graham? What do you expect?"

Myrddin's gaze fell on each person in the church. "This is why King Arthur has returned. To ask the hearts of his countrymen what it is they truly believe about God and His place in this world. Is it a miracle you want? Is it? Then behold a miracle!"

Suddenly the various doors around the church building exploded inward, and police officers emerged through each one. Arthur instinctively leapt to his feet and raised Excalibur.

Ponsonby marched down the center aisle at the side of a man with a roly-poly body and ruddy, Dickensian face. He was a police inspector named Cassidy.

"Nobody move!" Cassidy shouted, and then, in case someone hadn't caught on, "We're the police."

Ponsonby pointed to Arthur and said, "Shoot him if he moves even an inch."

The sight of Ponsonby made Arthur roar with anger.

Myrddin stepped in front of him, and in a tone that sharply contrasted with the commotion around them, said simply, "Remember the lesson. Put away the sword. This is not why you've come. The day will be won by miracles, not might."

Arthur cried out in frustration, "Then God grant me the strength for one more miracle!"

With both hands he raised Excalibur and drove its point into the stone altar. Steel screamed against stone as the blade went deeper and deeper. The veins on Arthur's neck stood out with the effort, and he grunted as the blade struck bottom. Then he stood back and admired his handiwork. Excalibur's jewelled hilt and a few inches of steel were all that showed above the altar.

CHAPTER 38

A shocked silence followed. Then Arthur smiled, knelt, and silently prayed.

Myrddin reached for the sword's handle and gave it a tug; first as a playful gesture, then a second time as a real attempt to withdraw the sword. It wouldn't budge. He looked at Graham and Adrian and smiled. "Behold your miracle."

The spell was broken, and everyone started to talk at once. Inspector Cassidy spluttered, "Well, one doesn't see that very often."

"It's a trick," Ponsonby declared. "It's a ruse to throw us off."

"Throw you off from what? What was the purpose of barging into my church like this?" Graham asked, trying to get some order to the moment.

Ponsonby stepped forward, still keeping his eye on the sword in the stone. "He's here to arrest your son and your lunatic on several different charges. Need we list them all right now?"

Adrian stood up at his pew. "Then Inspector Cassidy will have to arrest Mr. Ponsonby as well."

Cassidy was perplexed. "On what charges, young man?"

"Bribing public officials, for starters," Adrian replied.

"That's quite an accusation," Cassidy said stiffly.

"This deluded and ungrateful young man thinks he saw something incriminating on my computer at home," Ponsonby puffed. He grinned confidently. "It's all a mistake, and he certainly doesn't have any proof."

Adrian reached into his shirt pocket and pulled out a computer disk. "All the evidence is on this disk. It's a complete record of Ponsonby's payoffs, including a group of bank transfers made by modem tonight."

"He's bluffing!" Ponsonby sneered. "He broke in and stole that disk from my office!"

Adrian shook his head. "How could I break into a house

where I was living? There's nothing illegal about that, is there, Inspector?"

Cassidy groaned. "This is getting awfully complicated, Ponsonby."

Suddenly a bright flash went off, then another. Everyone looked around in the direction of the light, near the main doors. A photographer stood next to Andy Samuelson, the tabloid reporter who'd chased after Arthur at the airport. "Smile, everybody," Samuelson said.

Another flash went off.

"Who are you?" Ponsonby demanded.

"Andy Samuelson with the *Sun*, or the *Star*, or maybe the *Mail*, depending on who'll pay me the most for this story." He gestured to Malcolm and Jeff. "I've been chasing these Yanks all over the countryside to get some snaps of King Arthur. But if there's corruption and bribery to go with it, all the better!"

Ponsonby's face went crimson while Cassidy's went pale.

"I can see the headlines now. ARTHUR RETURNS TO BRITAIN TO SAVE CHURCH AND EXPOSE CORRUPTION!" Samuelson said gleefully, then to the photographer: "Get a few pictures of that sword in the stone. Front page stuff!"

Cassidy held up his hands. "That's it. Everybody comes to the police station. We'll sort this whole thing out down there!"

"I think," Malcolm said quietly, "I may want to make a call to the American embassy."

CHAPTER 39

A full-blown argument filled the small interrogation room at the Glastonbury Police Station.

"Even as evidence, it's not admissible. It was obtained by illegal means!" Ponsonby shouted at Cassidy.

Red-faced, Cassidy shook the printout of the disk's contents at Ponsonby. "Admissible or not, I want an explanation of this!" The printout was a complete list with the names of city and county officials and inspectors, account numbers, and substantial sums of money that had changed hands.

Three of the officials, who'd been dragged out of bed and stood dazed and sleepy, jumped into the argument simultaneously. "I don't know anything about this. . . . Where's my lawyer? . . . I never took a single penny . . ."

The waiting area was within earshot of the shouts. Samuelson scribbled notes on a pad and laughed to himself. "Nothing like the sound of grown men covering their bases."

"Will you really print this story?" Graham asked him.

Samuelson looked at Graham as if he'd just landed from another planet. "You better believe it. King Arthur, the church, the scandal . . . classic British journalism."

A door down the hall slammed, muffling the arguing voices. Cassidy's footsteps rang heavy in the hall. "They'll be at it all night. You're all free to go. Reverend Peters, I'd like you and your son to come back tomorrow morning to answer some questions about what happened at Ponsonby's manor."

"What about him?" Myrddin asked, hooking a thumb towards Arthur.

Arthur, arms folded, leaned against the soda machine. The contrast of a man dressed for the sixth century against the red and white lights and buttons of a dispenser made quite a picture.

"I'll deal with him some other time. He's the least of my worries," Cassidy said. From the interrogation room, it sounded as though a chair had been thrown over. "Back to the playpen," he said and stormed off.

"I want interviews with all of you," Samuelson announced as everyone stood to leave.

"Oh, please," Anne yawned. "We're going home now."

"I don't think we'll want that kind of press coverage," Graham said politely.

Samuelson smiled endearingly. "It's to your advantage, you know. The more exposure there is for your church, the more interest there'll be in restoring it."

Graham considered the point. "You're right. Let's talk tomorrow."

"And just think of all the revenue that'll be generated by people who'll want to see the mysterious sword in the stone altar," Samuelson added.

The idea hadn't occurred to Graham, but he had to admit it was true.

"How about you Yanks? Care to give me an exclusive about your adventure with King Arthur?"

Malcolm and Jeff glanced at each other. "No comment," they said.

At their cars in front of the police station, a silence fell on the seven of them as they realized they were saying good-bye.

"You'll be staying in the area to sightsee, I assume," Graham said hopefully to Malcolm and Jeff.

"I think so. No point coming all this way and not visiting for a while," Malcolm replied.

"Come for tea," Anne said. "We'll expect you tomorrow at four."

"Delighted." Malcolm smiled, then turned to Adrian. "What about you, Adrian? Will you be there?"

Adrian looked sheepishly at his parents. "I don't know. Will I?"

"It's your choice," Graham said. "We'd be happy to have you home again."

"Then I'll be there," Adrian said.

"Good," Jeff responded. "Maybe you can show me what guys our age do for fun around here."

"Myrddin, I want to talk to you about all of this. There are things I don't understand," Graham declared.

Myrddin raised an eyebrow. "For example?"

"I thought you said the point wasn't to save Christ Church."

"Saving Christ Church wasn't the point," Myrddin affirmed. "But isn't it just like God to go ahead and save it anyway. That was your miracle."

Graham agreed. "We'll expect you and Arthur for tea as well, you old lunatic."

The Peters family crawled into Graham's mini and waved as they drove away.

Jeff yawned and stretched. "Well, I guess we should go back to the inn now, right?"

"I guess so." Malcolm took a few steps towards his car, then realized that Arthur and Myrddin weren't following.

Jeff said, "Myrddin?"

Myrddin and Arthur were deep in a whispered counsel. Myrddin nodded, then addressed Malcolm. "We have to go to my cottage, and then there's one more mission, if you're willing."

CHAPTER 40

Dawn offered a sliver of yellow on the horizon as Malcolm pulled the car to a halt. Stretching out from the road, Salisbury Plain rose and fell through a deep fog in gentle slopes. The four men climbed out of the car.

Jeff shivered, having just awakened from the drive. "Okay, so what're we doing here?"

"Saying goodbye," Malcolm said.

"Goodbye! Who's leaving?"

Arthur looked wistfully at the field. He seemed older now.

"Oh," Jeff said sadly. "But he never met the queen or the prime minister."

"He did what he came to do," Myrddin said. "Things have been set into motion now that will not be stopped."

A silence fell on them like dew on the grass.

Abruptly, Arthur grabbed Malcolm's and Jeff's hands.

"God be with you," said Malcolm.

Jeff tried to swallow the lump in his throat. "See you later."

Arthur then embraced Myrddin and spoke gentle words that Jeff didn't understand. A tear slipped from his eye.

"I'll see you in my dreams," Myrddin smiled at Arthur.

Arthur turned his head suddenly as if he heard something out on the field. He moved in that direction, then raised his hand in salute to Malcolm, Jeff, and Myrddin.

"*Vale: oremus semper,*" Arthur said on the edge of a sigh.

"Farewell, let us pray always," Myrddin translated and waved back.

Jeff's expression was one of unmasked surprise. "Those are the same words Elizabeth said in the church ruin at Fawlt Line."

As Arthur was enshrouded in the thick fog, Myrddin pulled a horn, curved like a ram's horn, out from under his coat. He lifted it to his lips and blew as hard as he could. The mournful sound echoed across the plain.

The mist cleared for a moment, and they saw a shimmer of light as the sun flashed on armor and sword. A host of mounted knights, pennants flying in the breeze, approached Arthur. He climbed onto his horse and, for a moment, the watchers saw a marvelous king approaching his last battle. He turned and waved as the fog erased the vision from their sight. It was a dream.

"Or was it a dream?" Malcolm asked Myrddin as they drove back to Wellsbridge.

"A dream, perhaps. But whose dream? His or ours?" Myrddin said cryptically.

"Huh?" Jeff grunted from the back seat.

"Was Arthur a dream to us, or were we in Arthur's dream?"

Jeff adjusted to a more comfortable position. "I'm too tired to think about it," he muttered. "I just wanna know what'll happen to Arthur without Excalibur. He left it here. Doesn't he need it for his last battle?"

"Yes. But now he will face Mordred without it—and leave no room for doubt about the outcome," Myrddin replied sadly.

Malcolm tugged at his ear. "What about the sword in the stone altar? What will become of it?"

Myrddin shrugged. "I suppose it will stay there until the next Arthur can retrieve it."

"Yeah, right," Jeff said. "Maybe I'll try to pull it out when we get back."

"Maybe you should," Myrddin agreed.

Malcolm glanced over at the old man, reluctant to ask the next question. He did anyway. "How do you know all of this? Are you really Merlin?"

Myrddin smiled. "I'm simply a vessel of God, here to do His bidding."

Jeff thought on that for a few moments and obviously found it lacking as an answer. "Come on, tell us straight out. Are you Merlin or aren't you?"

Myrddin turned in the front seat to face him, his eyes sparkling. *"What do you believe?"*

CHAPTER 41

In the year following their adventure with King Arthur, Malcolm and Jeff kept an eye on the news from Britain. The Fordes—Alan, Jane, and Elizabeth—joined them in what became a small group of Arthurphiles, or so Malcolm christened them. They met and gossiped about the impact of Arthur's visit on the United Kingdom . . . which was significant.

Reports were sensational at first, as the nation dealt with the events from Wellsbridge. Christ Church became the center of attention. Initially, it was a curiosity to those who wanted to see the miraculous sword in the stone altar. Silliness soon followed as Arthur-sightings were claimed all over the world. Then, as often happens, the national and international press turned their fickle attention to other things, leaving room for a more serious phenomenon to take place.

Details were hard for the Arthurphiles to come by. But they heard that Christ Church became a source of a remarkable spiritual renewal that spread in churches throughout the country. Many said it was based on something more important than the sword or even an appearance of Arthur; it was a stronger and deeper movement that stirred "the childlike faith in the hearts of true Christian believers."

The Reverend Graham Peters, who grew from strength to strength to become a leading light in the Church of England, said in a rare letter to Malcolm that it wasn't only a childlike faith, but the actions resulting from that faith. "It's a choice we all have to make," he wrote. "We must know what we believe and then act on it." Malcolm thought that summed the experience up nicely.

Rumor had it that Graham was on the road to becoming the bishop of Bath and Wells, not through any personal cunning or political maneuvering, but because of his sincerity of heart and faith.

Shamed by the scandal over Christ Church, Ponsonby beat a

hasty retreat to Switzerland. He never returned to England. The archdeacon went into a forced early retirement after rumors persisted that his role in the whole affair was not entirely innocent.

Myrddin lived quietly in his cottage, resisting the attempts of some to turn him into a celebrity prophet.

As for Arthur, he met Mordred on the battlefield just as legend said. Though he knew he would die, he went forward anyway and succeeded in stopping Mordred's reign of terror. He knew what he believed and acted on it.

As for Excalibur, it remains in the stone altar even to this day, waiting for the once and future king to draw it out again.

Here's what other readers are saying about Paul McCusker's Time Twists novels . . .

"*This series is great. The plots are so exciting I could hardly put the books down.*"
—Erin D.

"*The books are wonderful! I stayed up until five A.M. reading one because it was so exciting!*"
—Katie S.

"*Your novel made me think. It made me ask questions. You also painted a picture in my mind while I was reading.*"
—Natalie R.

"*It was such an intriguing book I didn't even notice when I was turning the pages. The story has a good moral for kids.*"
—Philip B.

"*The book was very adventurous. . . . When I get a good book like this one, I just can't put it down.*"
—Jacob A.